Hollow Shores

Gary Budden

Hollow Shores

Gary Budden

dead ink

dead ink

First published in Great Britain in 2017 by Dead Ink, an
imprint of Cinder House Publishing Limited.

Paperback ISBN 9781911585251
Hardback ISBN 9781911585244

Printed and bound in Great Britain by Clays Ltd, St Ives
plc.

Cover illustration by Magdalena Szymaniec.

www.deadinkbooks.com

For my mother

'Perhaps it was his love of the mythical past, King Arthur and his knights, that brought him back. Or perhaps he felt as I did, that real change could only be affected in the place that you most understood: home.'

– Penny Rimbaud, *The Last of the Hippies*

'In small doses, melancholy, alienation, and introspection are among life's most refined pleasures.'

– Rebecca Solnit, *Wanderlust: A History of Walking*

'"Horror isn't everywhere," said Cushing. "But horror is somewhere every day."'

– Stephen Volk, *Whitstable*

'The world was almost translucent, as if we were already half among the dead. Nothing could be lovelier.'

– Robert Aickman, *The Attempted Rescue*

Contents

I.
Breakdown

My old man was a lorry driver, back in the eighties. He went all over and knows northern Europe like, he says, the back of his hand. I try and tell him it's all changed since his day, how the terrain morphs as we age. More black tar cutting through the land. More out-of-town supermarkets, retail parks and agribusiness. More post-EU regulations and migrants dodging the cops in Calais. Dad's map of the world ossified sometime around 1987, when the trees were closely packed together and strange shadows were cast on the ground.

I like to think his world was just that little bit wilder back then and I'm envious of that, hungry for whatever it was he saw in the woods. I yearn for days with a bit more breathing space, greater anonymity and more personality.

Dad talks about those years fondly, the days on the road before the kids and the divorce and the new family grounded him on the Essex coast. Proudly tells people how he can still roll a cigarette while driving, steering with his knees, how he saw some mighty odd things out on the road that you wouldn't believe. Straight-laced businessmen blowing each other in lay-bys. A head-on collision with a lorry carrying stationery supplies, staples and reams of paper spilling out like guts over the tarmac. A white fox just staring, yellow-eyed, and meeting his gaze, nonplussed, before he hit it.He talks about how it was tough but how he enjoyed the solitude and the anonymity life on the lanes gave him. There, he was just a driver. The mastodon roar of the traffic he found soothing, monotonous and dependable. To this day he's an excellent navigator, can get around by instinct alone. I've rarely seen him use a map, and satnavs don't really register on his radar.

It's funny how the memories of your family become your memories too. I have an image of swimming under my merchant navy ship, somewhere off the coast of South Africa, tanned men diving down, challenging themselves to curve under the ship and back up the other side. But this is a story Dad told me, about his dad. Grandad was the one who, at the point of bursting lungs and desperate to get to the surface, sees a circle of hammerheads and nearly drowns, arms churning the water in fright. Granddad, a man I never knew, transmitting his stories over the decades. Granddad survived the sharks and the deep dives under the trading ships, but he couldn't survive the Thames and drowned in its murk back in 1981, not yet an old man.

My uncle was a long-hauler too. He shut down the Blackwall Tunnel once when his twelve-wheeler's engine packed in. I think of him sometimes, stuck somewhere under the Thames, neither in Greenwich nor Tower Hamlets, choking off one of south England's busiest arteries. And here's me, who can't even drive.

Granddad's story is in the blood or something, genetic in a way an ability to drive clearly is not. My own biography involves no sharks, no long-hauls across Europe in winter. I have my own stories, though, of bloody knuckles and shaved heads, of spearbirds and skydancers, of a man coming down with the syndrome standing messianic in the busy streets of Jerusalem. But those are for another time.

There's a story of Dad's that niggles at me, one I come back to again and again, embellishing details, making minor edits. In those dead moments, when I'm staring out of a rain-streaked bus window on the way to work, crammed into the armpits of commuters on the Victoria line, or those days when the simplest of things seems a struggle, I think of Dad, a young man, lost in the Black Forest, a broken-down lorry and a fear he'd never get home. Dark descending and the bite of winter. Something out there, a shadow among shadows.

Like many men of his generation, Dad's cheery when discussing things that should be distressing or disturbing. Trauma is brushed off with a grin and the assertion *I could handle it, no bother*. Men didn't complain back then, he believes, nor should they now. He's old school and small-c conservative. But when he talks about Granddad sinking beneath the Thames and the circling sharks and that night in the Black Forest, there's perhaps a slight crease around the eyes, the tiniest hint of a grimace or wince showing that, below that surface of skin and bravado, some events do leave a lasting impact and, sometimes, things are just not OK.

When I lie in bed at night, listening to the traffic outside my window, I see the circling hammerheads. I think of bubbles escaping an open mouth and the grey waters of the Thames, my uncle stuck in his lorry somewhere far beneath. Imagine I hear a growl in the darkness. The story of that goat-legged thing and the solitary bird-tower, the arranged branches, the lonely woodcutter. The slow lowing of huddled cattle, the endless trees. It's a good yarn. I tell it in pubs to friends and acquaintances in London and Kent, my own interpretations and changes stitched into the story's fabric. I have this compulsion to tell it, something to puncture the humdrum, a little bit of the uncanny to enliven our dreary weekends. When Dad goes, I'll be the conduit for both him and Granddad.

*

Dad is doing one of his long-hauls over to Europe, the destination somewhere in Germany or Austria, requiring cutting through the Black Forest. It's winter and Christmas is coming. This is the last job before he heads back to Essex, to my mum and us. Some sort of bonus pay packet, overtime in order to stuff our stockings and buy Mum something decent for once. He feels bad that she's stuck at home with the kids, but what can you do? A man's got to work. He gets the ferry over the water, sets off through France, into Germany in a time before the Berlin Wall came down and the Cold War was still something discussed in the present tense. Were those times better or worse? I guess, at the very least, you had a sense of your place in the world.

Driving through that forest, he sees the slope of mountains carpeted with trees so dark they appear black, a few locals doing what they do along the roadside, cattle being herded in seeming slow motion to destinations unknown. A solitary woodcutter hefts an axe, fresh out of some Grimm tale and Dad thinks he can smell sawdust and pine resin. Dad imagines his own children – me, my sister Lisa – lost out in these woods, following breadcrumb trails and shivering with fright, coming to terms with their abandonment. Alone, tired and suffering from twelve hours straight on the road, his mind fills with leering lupine grins and bright menstrual reds, cannibal hags, confectionery dwellings. The forest, he knows, is a place where things happen. He passes a sort of wooden tower, its use opaque. Birdwatching, perhaps. A German hobby popular in these parts. A home for the lonely woodcutter.

Miles from anywhere, the engine packs in with a stutter and a sigh. The lorry grinds to a halt. It's getting dark already, the evergreens standing stern like angry patricians. It's cold and getting colder. Dad weighs up his options. The nearest town is at least five miles away. He doesn't know the terrain and his mind is full of sharp teeth and bleeding fur. The best plan, he decides, is to sleep in the lorry. Walk to the nearest town in the morning, flag down some passing motorist if he's lucky. Maybe the woodcutter will save him. Dad pulls his coat over himself, rubs his hands to try and stay warm, thinks of Christmas gifts for Mum and beds down for the night. His stomach growls but he has no food, and he shivers himself to sleep.

About three in the morning he wakes, breath pure white fogging up the windows, the moisture quick to freeze. There's ice on the *inside* of the cab. There's a chill in him that goes bone deep: it's all encompassing and his limbs now are dead wood, unresponsive. He's ready for the chop, unless he does something. He thinks of Granddad thrashing underwater in fright, forces himself awake and out of the lorry. Begins, ridiculously, doing star jumps, running on the spot, laps around the vehicle, anything to get the blood pumping and his temperature up. The woods are still and silent. He's thankful for his torch, its perfect line of light cutting through a blackness thick and tar-like, ready to consume the unwary.

Nothing but the closed ranks of the evergreens. No, on closer inspection, in a gap among the trees he can see small signs of humanity. A rough path, compressed pine needles and leaf litter. He thinks he hears something, sees what may be the light of a fire ahead. Curiosity overcomes fear. To this day, he'll claim he was half-delirious with cold and hunger and fatigue. He enters the woods. Feels the eyeless glares of the pines regard him from all sides, the prickly rustle of the pine needle carpet he walks on making him think, absurdly, of Christmas back in Essex. The torch beam is a single yellow line slashed across black tarmac. He thinks about all the impossible chains of events that lead to these moments in our lives.

He sees cut branches, arranged pyramid-like, a jerry-built temple. Like the skeleton of a tipi maybe, but festooned with plants and offerings. Sharp holly and bloody berries, some straw facsimile of a human being, pine boughs bent like the arms of crippled children. In the light of day festive and seasonal, but here, in this black night, in the depths of a fairytale forest, malignant and cancerous. Ahead, a faint orange fire-glow.

That's when he hears a kind of growling chuckle. His torch beam frantically scans the terrain, and maybe there's a hint of black fur approaching, the shadows thicker and darker in places than they should be. Dad staggers back, sees something goat-legged and red-tongued, a furred forest god grinning, and behind it androgynous beings of golden straw standing motionless amongst the evergreens. Hints of a blade, clawed fingers on curled hands. In that moment, he sees the thing he knows is impossible and utterly of this place: forest devil, horned god, punisher of the wicked. A warning for the children. The thing sees him, this English man from Essex, and seems to smile and flex its claws, and maybe it beckons him. And you know what? He feels the pull. To join this world and never come back. He knows, deep down, he is wicked. But he thinks of Mum alone and my sister sitting under a plastic pine tree.

This is when he runs, runs back to the road and leaves the lorry where it is: runs, walks and stumbles until he hits the next village five miles down the road and bangs on German doors for help and the assertion that this is the real world, not that world out there in the woods, where things he doesn't want to know about happen and are happening and will always happen.

He's quizzed by local police, is savvy enough to keep it simple and say he simply got lost and frightened. They find the lorry the next morning, ice on the inside. Call a mechanic who gets the job done. As he works, Dad scans the lines of evergreens and the path of trampled needles is not there. He hears, somewhere, a man chopping wood.

He quit the lorry driving soon after that, and then found Christianity in a big way, hit it like a drug. Mainlined the stuff. Mum says it was the guilt after he left us but I think it was something else. It's something I've never forgiven him for, and I know that the beginnings of that flight toward what he considers holy began with that thing that may have been a bear, a tree, a magnificent horned stag, but was not.

He doesn't want it, it embarrasses him. The story is mine now.

Gary Budden

II.
Saltmarsh

In the city he sees mainly i) green parakeets swarming in the trees of Gladstone Park ii) rot-legged pigeons the colour of exhaust fumes peppering the sky above Staples Corner and iii) jays that flit colourfully among the trees near the Jewish cemetery. The first two he hates, and the third he has a real fondness for.

It's holiday season and the marsh grass is jaundiced and sullen. Simon has left the boatyard behind, with its creaking rusted winches, fleece-wearing woodcutters and carved folk art, where boats bob on the creek with names like *Jack Orion*, *Georgie* and *Reynard*. Now he is thankfully alone, the town that fades out by the creek falling away behind him. The cold needles his skin and the sky is the blue of a blackbird's egg. The wind is sharp like flint. Electricity pylons march towards the murky waters of the Swale. The sunlight exposes all.

Yesterday, over a bad Skype connection, Simon's sister relayed breathy accounts of seeing not one, but two sea eagles in as many weeks on the broads between Norfolk and Lowestoft. A train rumbling through morning mist, sharp talons and a yellow beak. (She meant the white-tailed eagle.) He has never seen a sea eagle (white-tailed eagle) bar on his HD screen with a BBC presenter relaying the facts, figures and opinions. He is jealous of his sister for this, feels it's a sight that should be earned. It's not a bird for amateurs. He knows that to give himself the chance of even seeing such a bird he needs to be elsewhere; not in the city, not in the south east trudging through this saltmarsh along the Hollow Shore. Though, in this county, at the right time of year, he knows he can see the shore harriers with talons locked tight together spiralling down into the reeds. It's a sight that opens up parts of him not normally accessible. This year, he promises himself, he will take Adrianna to see them. They are rare and it hurts him to watch them.

Once he and Adrianna saw, through a smeared bus window, a white peacock treading the tarmac somewhere near Regent's Park, disrupting the traffic. He wonders briefly what happened to it and remembers the confused honking of the taxi drivers. Whether they were heading towards, or coming back from Victoria he can't remember.

He is not in East Anglia, yet the landscape here is similar. Intimidating flatness with too much space for the mind to wander. The haunting burble of curlews out on the mudflats, affecting still, despite the amount written about them. A boat of some sort (he's not a sailor) nose down in the creamy mud as if burrowing for lugworms. These are not broads, though, this patch between Faversham (his point of departure) and Whitstable (destination). What constitutes a 'broad', Simon wonders? Something to look up.

Seven miles ahead lies the fishing-cum-tourist town where, he knows, the cafes are already full (they have names like Samphire) and the pubs (Neptune, The Ship Centurion) are filling up, glasses stamped with the Shepherd Neame logo sloshing with amber liquid. He can already taste that pint, the pleasing decision between Spitfire, Whitstable Bay or Bishop's Finger. A bag of scampi fries too. It will be well-earned, the fractal patterns of mud that flow up his trousers the mark of honour to say, 'I have earned this drink.' It's a personal thing. Goals are important, no matter how arbitrary.

If you asked why he is out here on this saltmarsh, he would be hard-pressed to come up with an answer. He just feels the compulsion these days to connect town to town by foot – no car, bike or train providing enough significance.

To come into a new town on foot, the buildings slowly coalescing and condensing into a form that can be slapped with a useful postcode, is one of life's rarest pleasures. Sometimes an explanation is not needed when the truth is self-evident. He feels it, and therefore (for him at least) it is true. He'd like to think he's part of some form of mild rebellion. He's been trying to persuade John to come with him on one of these trips.

It does sound good when announced in pubs back in the city, where the perceptions of rural, provincial, anything other than exhaust fume and clogged carriage, is deemed luxurious and exotic. Simon once announced, half-cut on a Kentish ale now sold in London arts venues, 'I am being throttled by the M25.'

Adrianna hates his grandiose statements, but she dreams idly of leaving too. She thinks maybe the West Country, trips to the Mendips and Deer Leap, supping cider in Bath or Bristol. They've considered coming back to the somehow overcrowded rural parts of Kent; they both have family here. Simon feels the appeal, yet doesn't believe he can be one of *those people*. Maybe somewhere on the Sussex coast with the blue waters of the channel and local mackerel in a bun? Right now anywhere else would do. Home is no longer no home.

Home is a place where the skyline is stabbed by cranes, bent as if in prayer, diggers like mastodons whose wheels are slathered in London clay, half-built or half-demolished buildings (he finds it hard to tell these days) that he'd describe as skeletons or shells if he could consider anything living ever using them.

He and his friends, Adrianna who he thinks of as his wife but not his wife, are now cash *and* time poor. He resents that a few drinks with John on a Wednesday night can set him back as much as thirty quid. Resenting the cost of your spare time, a terrible thing.

He says he's forgotten how to live in anywhere other than the cramped metropolis, and that, perhaps, is why he is here on these cold saltmarshes when he could instead be at home with Adrianna, in bed sipping coffee and reading the arts section of the *Guardian*.

The wind stings his eyes. Two polite cyclists, mud spinning off their wheels like a Catherine wheel, say 'Hello' and 'Good morning' politely as they pass Simon on their way (he assumes) for a brunch and coffee in one of the new boutique cafes of Faversham creek. They recede into the distance and Simon stops to look at, and photograph, a green, white and wasp coloured Environment Agency sign attached to metal fencing warning of the numerous ways to die out here: unguarded culverts, deep water, slippery surfaces, deep mud, underwater obstructions, etc.

Simon wonders, briefly, where and when samphire grows (and how to cook it) and wishes he could identify the sullen plant life he's stamping on. If only I had a garden, he thinks, then I could begin to get to grips with all this. He wants the feel of seed in his hand. Would the parakeets back home eat that scattered seed? Hopefully not. He has a book on organic gardening, in a bag underneath the spare bed, along with his old copies of *Magnesium Burns* and *Punk Positive* that he never reads but cannot let go of.

This garden in his mind has a simple birdbath, discreet nesting boxes nailed to the tree (his garden needs at least one tree, preferably fruiting, preferably apple) and a squirrel-proof feeder to attract dunnocks and goldfinches. He plans on a ceramic recreation of the face of the green man, placed somewhere to surprise the visitor when their eyes finally alight on it. He would also like a sheela na gig (would visitors find the exaggerated vulva off-putting?).

His garden would also contain one of those tinkly metal things that chime in the breeze. That could be good. Simon thinks of his favourite animals: i) narwhal/sea-unicorn ii) chocolate and butterscotch pine marten and iii) simple umber fox/Reynardine. If motifs of these animals could be woven into the design of his garden, all the better. Adrianna mocks what she calls his 'hippy shit', and he can see her point.

Once, at a festival somewhere in a field outside of Winchester, where he and Ade met Jess, he saw a gypsy-traveller type selling wicker women in figures of restful repose, a Gaia-type addition to any flower bed. He found them rather striking, but thought it best to keep his thoughts to himself. Could see Adrianna's piss-take face and could hear John's condemnation. Simon is getting older and listens to more and more music featuring acoustic guitars and fiddles. He watches *Springwatch* with a passion, and the number of jumpers he owns is increasing. He never thought he'd go this way, but finds it all strangely pleasing.

At present, he knows little about soil rotation, whether his loam and humus would be alkali or acid, and wonders if eggshell really is a good addition to a compost mulch. What is the best brand of shovel, trowel, fork? He feels a kind of hatred towards the mild-mannered TV presenters of the BBC (one of whom, he discovered, moonlights as a successful romance novelist). Simon doesn't want to be one of those English people, discussing the merits of different brands of bonemeal in provincial garden centres, in a county where the St George's cross flaps constantly in the wind. But he does want a garden.

He can see a number of false starts, but the journey, not the destination, is the point, right?

So much to learn.

He likes to find areas of mild interest but nothing to shout about, then connect the two by footpaths seldom trod. Photograph the burrowing boats and rusting detritus obscured by reeds. Upload the pictures to a blog, along with a modest amount of text. Share amongst other landscape enthusiasts (there are many online behind their computers in cramped flats). He is part of, he supposes, a kind of community.

The curlew calls again. He pauses, checks his phone. Buzzings and exclamation marks concerning some breaking outrage. A message from Adrianna wishing he has a good day and asking what time he thinks he may be home. She's only back in Faversham; they are staying with her parents for the holiday period. He'll hop on the train back (about a five-minute trip) later. There are a few favourites and one retweet for the picture of the Environment Agency sign he's uploaded to Twitter. He theorises his use of the word 'culvert' helped in this.

He is walking now at a steady pace, his face bitten by the wind but sweating slightly inside his thick green coat. Simon walks parallel to a narrow strip of water, the Swale, separating here (mainland) from there (Deadman's Island). Over there are prisons, boxing hares, economic hardships and stories of monsters in the reeds the locals call the Sons of Cain. Somewhere on the island is the skull of Grey Dolphin (a horse).

There are approximately 5,000 islands dotted around the coast of the UK. As he walks along the Swale, Simon counts all the islands he has visited:

i) Scilly Isles with Dad, aged 9/10, approx. 1989; St Mary's, Tresco, Samson. Helicopter journey from Penzance.

ii) Isle of Wight, rained-out camping trip with Adrianna, 2011.

iii) Farne Islands, aged 11/12, Dad again, approx. 1991, memorable for being dive-bombed by nesting terns and watching bridled guillemots.

iv) Lindisfarne? Will check with Dad. He remembers an abbey, somewhere.

v) Deadman's Island, tracking Grendel and Grey Dolphin. Boxing hares on the fields. Possible sighting of a spearbird.

vi) Vartiosaari, off the coast of Helsinki. Adrianna found very affecting, 2012. Picked wild blueberries, watched mating great crested grebes and found a troll church.

vii) Suomenlinna (originally Sveaborg/Viapori); inhabited former sea fort off Helsinki. Chain of six islands in total, once Swedish defence against the Russians. A restaurant where Adrianna gingerly ate reindeer.

viii) Isle of Dogs (of course).

ix) Fish Island, East London (named after surrounding streets Bream, Roach, Dace etc.) They used to like to drink down that way, before things changed.

x) Isle of Man, sometime during early teens. Indistinct memory of a cat with no tail and watching black guillemots through a new pair of binoculars that Dad had bought him for Christmas.

Not a stunning list, but it could be worse.

He and John have a plan, of sorts, to find passage to Deadman's Island in the estuary, lying over the water from the Hollow Shore. The difficulty in getting there is becoming part of the point – the pointless pilgrimage – almost every aspect of it becoming the cliché of some hoary old ghost story. They must arrange private passage with a local fisherman, who will take them to the island, as well as securing permission from Natural England. It's a bird sanctuary built on disease and suffering. The place appeals to his curiosity and John's morbidity. They want to find the diseased bones of the dead Frenchmen rising from the mud. Remnants of the prison hulks (whose inmates he can only ever picture as Ray Winstone in a BBC Dickens adaptation). And so on. He knows his Twitter followers would go nuts for it. Adrianna finds it macabre and is not interested.

Simon passes on the path a group of men and women, six in total, swilling strong lager from cans that bear the image of a European bison (the wisent).

They speak a language that may be Polish but he is hopelessly unsure. He wants to ask them what they're up to, in a friendly way, but decides against it. Attempts a 'Good morning', like with the cyclists back near Faversham, but is met with silence. They continue until the saltmarsh swallows them and they disappear. A herring gull shrieks.

Simon pauses to lean against the concrete flood defence that borders this part of the path, rolls and lights a cigarette. He looks over the waters of the Swale to Deadman's Island. The water is choppy, the colour of silt and slate, freezing. He feels the desire to push on, to be back among eating drinking people and out of the stinging wind. The sun is blinding him and he wishes he'd brought sunglasses like Adrianna suggested.

By his feet, he notices a few orange-brown mushrooms pushing up through the grass. Another thing to add to his list: mycology. Wouldn't it be nice to forage the occasional meal, with the added danger of vomiting and stomach cramps.

The curlew cries, like bubbles escaping from a mouth submerged.

He is meeting John in the pub. His oldest friend is also down in Kent visiting family. It's that time of year.

Though they often see each other in London, this is a good excuse for Simon to do this walk, stretch the legs and mind, and to sit in the warmth of his favourite pub, The Old Neptune, sipping Shepherd Neame ale by a crackling fire, listening to the Irish landlord and looking at the glass containers of pickled whelks sitting behind the bar. No one ever seems to buy them. Often, the hippy ex-road-protester guy, Fen, can be found propping up the bar. Fen lived in a friend's shed for a decade and wrote a book (self-published, obviously) suggesting the UK is, in fact, a buried giant. Or a cherubic being in flight (if you look *really* hard). Whitstable is the centre of the Gog-Magog axis, Fen says on the videos on his YouTube channel. It sounded good but sadly, Simon realised, probably didn't mean much.

Sun reflects like quicksilver off the mudflats, making them look carved from stone. Simon pauses to examine a sign. The bird and plant life to be found here on South Swale nature reserve. Brent geese, buntings, red-breasted mergansers.

Above him tower the pylons in a domineering sexual pose. He thinks he hears a crackling sound.

He walks with no other humans in sight. What a luxury to be alone on this packed island.

A pub, lonely out here on the marshes, takes form. The Shipwrights Arms, famous in local lore for its spectral-star, the ship spectre. The ghosts here crowd and whisper like the reeds.

It's a pub he has never, in fact, visited. Too local, he used to assume, but perhaps this trip will be the time that he ventures in there. With mud-spattered trousers, binoculars and thick green coat it seems more acceptable somehow, rather than settling down with a pint and crisps as an obvious Londoner, or DFL (Down From London), as they are known.

He feels disconnected. So, perhaps, this walk is an act of penance, a pilgrimage in a secular age. He could have driven, after all (about fifteen minutes) or gotten the train (service every half hour, five-minutes journey time), whereas this walk will take, roughly, four hours.

On foot, the world becomes a bigger place. To be in the places you only normally stare at through the train window feels revelatory. Like stepping into the background somehow, text tumbling over the margin and off the page, wading into the painting, whatever; it's that feeling of being *elsewhere* that is so compelling. And finding *elsewhere* at home? He never thought it possible.

He trudges on. Out on the water bobs a boat so rusted it cannot possibly be in use. Back at the creek he'd looked at the boats clearly inhabited, rainbow-coloured, evoking the lyrics of folk songs. Who were these people?

He's heard the stories about the raves on the marshes. His younger cousin Teddy has done it. An eight-mile schlep back home through mud and mire, still pilled-up and happy as the summer sun came up over Deadman's Island. Simon envies him.

Though didn't he do just the same? Just in different places. He thinks of home that is becoming not home, and a real pang grips his insides. Bits of that life that he does not regret, but that he cannot return to, come in a tidal flood:

i) London Bridge, summertime, dawn. The sight of the sun appearing to light the Thames. The breathtaking moment when he truly knew where he was, and he was in London.

ii) Visiting the Cable Street mural with Adrianna for the very first time; drizzle in the air and grey skies and a bit of tiny pride in this city that was home.

iii) Him and his old friend Sally, in the wooded outskirts of a festival near Northampton, high as kites and swearing in the trees they could discern anthropoid figures; wodewose, spriggan, green man, horned god, etc.

iv) An impromptu picnic with Adrianna in Springfield Park. Summer drizzle forcing them to take shelter under foliage. Orthodox Jewish wedding at one end of the park, lads dealing weed at the other. They sipped cava from plastic flutes and ate hummus with Turkish bread.

v) The Balustrade, NYE 2003.

Simon, Adrianna, John – though they've knocked it on the head now, they're all au fait with what goes in these marginal spaces. Psy-trance and drum'n'bass in the woods in Wiltshire. Heavy bass and bowel-churning dub up in the Brecon Beacons. Countless nights of piercings, dreadlocks and heavy, heavy hardcore in The Balustrade.

The path begins slowly to become more and more regulated, the buildings of the small hamlet of Seasalter appearing. He walks for a good two miles along the bleak shoreline thinking not of the place where he is now, in winter in biting wind, but of a place that no longer exists, in a past that he misses.

The Balustrade up in East London is long gone, bulldozed and converted into i) luxury flats ii) a franchise coffee shop and iii) an arts space. Its destruction was one of those nails in the coffin that made him and Adrianna consider jumping ship. The place where he and John spent many, many nights, where Simon met Adrianna, a place that he wishes still exists. It *was* an arts space, a creative space, a space for people. But not the right kind of people. Untaxable and in the way of progress.

Which means he and the woman he loves were not, and possibly are not, the right kind of people. Simon always felt all those commonplace emotions as a young man; I don't fit in, the world is not for me, I feel an outcast, etc. It always seemed too obvious a point to give any serious contemplation. Out here, on the edges of this saltmarsh, covered in mud and listening to the burbling of the curlew, it feels correct. If he is being strangled by the M25, then his memories of the city are now being bulldozed and redeveloped.

His phone buzzes in his pocket and snaps him back into the moment. Sometimes his leg spasms even when there is no phone there, when no one is trying to contact or communicate with him. It's one of those modern things, John assures him. This one is real though.

Here Now, from John.

Twenty minutes, Simon replies.

Simon picks up the pace, a slight dampness now under the armpits that he enjoys and considers honest. He passes what look like the tyre treads for a tank rusting next to silent beach huts with names like *Oystercatcher* and *Curlew Cottage*. A few houses jut up onto the beach itself and he crunches across the pebble and shingle to pass them. A Union Jack flutters high up a white pole. Simon shakes his head.

He can feel a new town beginning to take shape. Dog walkers begin to appear, a pair of young and eager joggers jog past, older couples arm in arm brace against the wind as they take a walk. Back to reality.

He passes the golf course and thinks, as always, how the land should be taken and rewilded. Give it back to the curlews and turnstones, take it from the men with silly trousers.

Finally, the pub comes into view. Isolated outpost against the sea. The Old Neptune. Simon has been drinking here on and off for twenty years now and it's still his favourite.

He pushes the door, steps inside. Warmth and that wonderful smell of lager and human beings hits him. The fire is going and John has commandeered a table to make full use of the warmth. Above the fire is a stylised portrait of Ian Dury.

'Took your time,' says John with a grin. He's been ripping beermats.

'What are you having?' Simon asks.

*

Old Fen sits at the bar dreaming of the fallen giant that lies beneath Kent. The Irish barmaid polishes glasses, pickled shellfish preserved behind her in glass containers.

Simon and John clink their pint glasses in greeting. Outside the sky is still sharp and clear. Simon can see a few gulls pecking at a discarded and congealing bag of chips out on the stones. The tide is out, flat mud stretching towards Deadman's Island. Beyond that, over the estuary, Southend, Essex, the rest of England.

'Good walk?' asks John. He wears a new Harrington, gleaming boots, dark blue jeans.

'Yeah, it was good, gets the blood pumping and all that.'

'It's nice being down here, even at this time of year. I do miss it at times.'

'Me too. But I think we forget all the reasons why we left.'

'The Union Jacks and the boredom.'

'We couldn't wait to get away, remember? The fucking small town bullshit. All we did was burn wood on the beach and smoke ourselves stupid and plan trips up to London.'

'At least we had the beach.'

'We did.'

They sit and talk for a few hours, cocooned in the warmth of the pub, of how each other's families are doing, of how Adrianna is, how John is doing since his breakup. How Old Fen has propped up the bar since as long as they can remember. There's a gig coming up in London that they plan to be at, the last night at The Stockwell Arms before the developers are let loose. They laugh and make light of it. Neither admits the discomfort they feel. These places, these are their shared stories.

'Remember The Balustrade?' says John, booze fuelling nostalgia.

'Fucking hell what a place,' says Simon.

'Where you met Ade wasn't it?'

'Yeah.'

And Simon thinks how twelve years have passed and how the present became the past. He wants to tell his friend about his ideas for gardens, about the trips to the Mendips he has yet to take yet that are so vivid in his mind they feel like cherished memories, how he needs to get out of the city, change, move on, before the whole world he knew gets knocked down. It all sounds like so much bitter moaning when aired; and as such, often, the conversation remains perfunctory. They retell stories of the things they did and struggle to imagine what they now will do.

John gets up, stretches his arms and rubs a hand over his cropped hair, and heads to the bar for another pint. He flirts with the Irish barmaid. He has a charisma that Simon has always envied. The pub is filling up with Kentish locals, an old man with an old dog, gleaming middle-class couples who must be down, like them, from the city. The fire crackles.

Old Fen smiles to himself and sips his pint.

Gary Budden

III.
Baleen

There was all the stuff you'd expect: heart lungs liver kidneys etc. Baleen, thick and numerous like bristles on an old paintbrush. But nothing in the gut, half-digested and smelling of pricey French perfume. Empty intestines, they said, unraveled for half a mile. It was running on nothing. No signs of malnutrition or malnourishment, no pocks or blemishes suggesting deficiencies, no barnacles like aggressive teen acne, no scuttling whale lice, pale and piercing. As if the model had arrived straight off the factory line without once being used. An idea of a whale.

When it happened I was drinking a lot, watching popular dramas through my digibox and not feeling as bad as I should have done about being laid off.

The guy who found the whale was one of those motivated joggers in tight Lycra running along the shore. He liked to get up early, he said in the local paper, and be alone with the herring gulls and piles of rotting bladderwrack. *The crunch of shingle beneath my feet. It's so peaceful at dawn.*

I'd seen the dawn on the coast myself, but from the improper perspective and coming at it from the wrong direction. Never gotten up to see the pink glow, only ever stayed awake long enough for it to creep up on me. People don't respond to those stories in the same way, and I wonder how I'd have been portrayed if I had found the carcass.

Leviathan, beached whale, signifier of something I've yet to put my finger on. It's not that beachings are uncommon on this coast. A pod of pilot whales, in sympathetic solidarity, left themselves out to dry up on Dunlin Point. That was in '96. Bottlenose dolphins too, so numerous it hurt to think about it, committed mass suicide in St Michael's Bay, like they'd all decided it was just too much effort to keep going. That was '02. I knew the story from Victorian times about a sperm whale washed ashore near the town six miles down the coast; opening it up, an intrepid scientist stepped into the thing's heart only to slip and end up drowning in whale blood.

Our whale was ninety feet long, a pristine and unblemished sky blue. It was alone. The morning it happened, I noticed a commotion outside. More people than usual, kids with sticks they used to prod and poke. The weather was clear but cold, heading toward winter. I pulled on my thick green coat, mud-crusted boots I'd bought on offer from Sports Direct, made sure my iPhone was charged. Always worth grabbing a few pics. The coast along the Hollow Shore, bleak though it is, is always photogenic.

I crossed the road, listening to the cries of the herring gulls up among the chimneys, ducked down the little alley that wound past a beached wooden boat and onto the beach. Shingle crunched underfoot – it was nice, the jogger was right – and already a crowd of the townspeople and journalists surrounded the whale, cameras flashing like they were a group of tourists at the Louvre.

And what a sight. Even as the birds pecked at its flesh, it was majestic. It made life in this provincial, salt smelling town, seem all the worse. Here was a reminder of what life could be, how fucking grand the world was capable of being, how I had just been let go from Pfizers as they wound up the business and was drinking my way through a dwindling stash of savings watching HBO dramas.

There was a recession on. The council made all the right noises but nothing happened. The story got into the national papers, a wind-blown journalist for BBC South East pontificating to camera as a herring gull tore off a strip of blubber in shot behind him. But there was no money, they said. Nothing spare to haul the carcass away. A travesty, shouted the scientists and naturalists. This thing was, after all, an anomaly. But it costs tens of thousands to haul a whale away, even one so empty and pure.

As the days and weeks went by, with the stench increasing (a mix between that rotting bladderwrack, abattoir, open sewer and fungal infection), I'd think about its baleen and the strokes of a giant's brush on a canvas as wide as the sky. I wondered where it had come from, and why. I found stories about whales that were the last of their species, singing a song that would never find an audience. Or reports from men with expensive equipment far out on the open sea, about whale song recorded matching no known records. I wondered if our whale was one of a kind, some chance mishap of whale miscegenation, doomed to beach on the south coast of England and never be understood. I could sympathise with that.

A kind of rogue science set in, looting the booty. I wasn't above it myself. There was money to be had. I hacked off the flukes that first night. No CCTV on the beach, only kids smoking weed sat around crackling driftwood fires, listening to the pop of heated pebbles. I sold the flukes to a collector on the dark web who paid enough money to buy me a few more months. I felt bad but, like I said, there was a recession on. I took a chunk of flesh for myself, while it was still fresh, and fried it up in my small kitchen. It was tasty, if chewy. For some reason I thought it would taste of fish.

Each morning I'd head out and check on our whale's progress. Death has its own energy. A micro-ecology feeding boiling masses of maggots and flies, the gulls, waders, crows and more that fed on the insects, flesh and thick skin. The peregrine I saw take an unwary gull. The slithering things and barking foxes at night.

The whale got its own Twitter account, fuelling a thousand shared photographs of the wonder of decomposition. Some thought it a sign of salvation, others doom, and so the whale fed us too, allowing us to project what we wanted onto its degraded form.

One morning, the whale now just shreds of flesh hung over a bone frame, I headed to the beach and saw a man who had scolded me for throwing stones at cans the previous summer. He was sitting on a wooden bench, staring out over at the carcass and the flat sea behind. I don't think he recognised me.

It's a disgrace, I said, close, so he would hear.

What's that?

Children have to play around here, I said.

I carried on towards the whale. Gulls took flight at my approach. The smell of rot everywhere. Flies were buzzing, a dirty encircling halo.

IV.

Ren

You can find Ren in the underpass under the screeching trains, that place where the black lake forms after heavy rain. He's there most days. He's lean and bony, his clothes in need of detergent, frayed denim smudged and stained. He smokes cheap shag tobacco and his fingertips are jaundice-yellow. He smells musty and of musk, is damp like the overgrown plants and the rotting nettles. He'll stand there and speak to the homeless taking temporary shelter, alarming the buggy pushers who pass Ren and the shiny sleeping bags, onto the cafe for coffee and carrot cake. He told me of how a group of ten, all leather jackets and lip piercings and tattoos, stood there for a long while guarding suitcases and bags of clothes. Just another one of those London things, he says. I like him and he is disgusting. His long sharp teeth are nicotine brown and I say he should book himself in for the deep clean. As if that's ever going to happen, he says.

In the early summer, all is moist and warm, sunshine and showers bringing the world back to life. Cow parsley up the embankments, nettles and dock leaves, burst of bluebells if you know where to look, green light where before there was only grey. This is Ren's favourite time.

People forget how quiet London can be. When it's me and Ren wandering the streets around the Downs on a wet Tuesday afternoon in half-term, past the small traveller site, the empty school, the endless flats and houses that prove someone must be there, it feels like we're the only two sentient beings in the world. The wet air dampens down birdsong. By January of each year I have forgotten how green parts of the city can be and how they are home to so much more than us. It's my home as much as yours, says Ren. He's a meat eater, from the country originally, but now has developed more of a taste for fried chicken bones and dripping doner meat. I saw him once take an orange-red box straight from an overflowing bin, still half-full, devour greedily the greasy cold contents. Shame to see things go to waste, he says. People starve in this city. So much food just waiting to be taken. I say he's a parasite and a sponger and all he does is light another cigarette and deepen the stains on his teeth and fingers. He has a glamour I can't deny. He says he's a survivor.

I know so little about him. All I know is he can be found in the underpass when rain brings the black lake. He can be found on the benches by the alkies enjoying the sweet rot of the park as an area designated untamed grows and grows to tempt back the dying butterflies. When I sit with him I sneeze and my nostrils clog with pollen or perhaps pollution and I can smell life and death, and so can Ren, but he feels it, I feel, in a way that I do not. He is skinny and frayed, stained and pungent, rust-haired with a burnt-umber beard. He is a feast for the senses. He is good company. He admires my raven hair, my blue eyes and lips he describes like wine.

Hollow Shores

I don't bring my dog to our meetings. Ren doesn't like dogs. When the rest of the city is rushing by and panicking, we sit on the bench in the downs and we talk of other things. He tells me about his love of drone and doom and folk and I enjoy that. With only endless time, he knows so much. He implies he's from money and that explains his grace. He promises me things I know he can never deliver; a different life, a trip to the mountains. He flashes his sly smile with his stained teeth and I want to believe him. He's a rake. Useless, a liar, a dream you want to believe in.

The trains rumble and scream overhead. I can smell the compost heaps. Plants grow in this park in the city. It's here I sit, most days, with Ren.

V.

Greenteeth

Nell sits on her bench. Hair like duckweed and a coat the colour of bilge, textured like algae. She must be hot. Her little black dog dozes in the sun by her feet. She's drinking from a can clenched in a fist, that chemical super-strength stuff that rots you from the inside out.

Two cyclists speed by, tight Lycra arses on their way to Walthamstow. I hear the hooting yelp of a moorhen from somewhere in the green at the canal's edge. A bit further up, nestled in the gentle curve of the navigation, I can see PK and Jess lounging on cheap patio chairs by their scruffy boat, *Ginny*. I wave to them. PK, armed with a smouldering spliff and decked out in an aggressively political T-shirt, seems not to notice. Jess, her light brown arms rippling with sylvan tattoos, sips a bottle of Sol and waves back. It's Sunday.

Tom climbs up onto the roof. *Peg* rocks gently, rippling the water. He extends a hand down to me, says, 'Come up love,' and as I half-climb and am half-hauled onto *Peg*'s roof, I watch Nell staring into the navigation, seeing nothing.

*

Think of the city in layers. Too often measured in urban sprawl, width, diameter, population density. Rarely in depth, in height. The vertical, the submerged, and all those bits in between. I live in a sunken city, a place interstitial with coots and cormorants and rats. Not Top-London or London-Under. London-in-between, neighbour to Canada goose and heron. But even here, we're fighting for space.

There is London, its streets and bookies, pubs and gastropubs and caffs and bakeries. There is Top-London; the glassy point of the Shard, the thrusting glass cocks with cute names that hide their malice, the chimneys at Battersea, the upper reaches of the beautiful brutalist blocks, and the ever-present cranes. There is London-Under, a realm of Roman relics and burnt soil where the trains rumble, commuters crush and, I'm sure, troglodytes gather in forgotten tunnels performing rituals to obscene gods.

My London-in-between – there are so many – is the canal network, fighting mildew in winter, coaxing cherry tomatoes and herbs from plastic pots come summer. Sunken veins just below the dirty city streets, pleasant remnants from an industrial past that helped ruin the world.

I am mobile in a way that is somehow acceptable, even romanticised. It's come as a surprise. If I tried this lifestyle on land they'd send the bailiffs in, before turning my life into a Channel 4 documentary. Maybe it's only a matter of time before we get labelled water gypsies and the resentments begin to build. A strange mix, jealousy and contempt.

Still, that's the future and that's never been a very clear place to me. I never thought I'd be water-bound, watching the spear-strike of a grey heron whilst sipping instant coffee, listening to the splash of something heavy entering water as I try to sleep on our floating home. It's just me and Tom on the boat, a cruiser we christened *Peg Powler*. A name I dredged from the depths of childhood. It seemed to fit. Tom wanted *Ondine*; I called him pretentious.

What we lack in space, I hope, we make up for in freedom. There *is* something to be said about waking up on a May morning by Markfield Park, poking a head out of the hatch to the screaming of swifts catching insects by the mouthful as they swoop over the reservoirs, drawn by boiling clouds of insect life. The sun on my skin, the splash of a landing mallard, the soft whir of passing cyclists' wheels. I can sit up on deck rolling a smoke and simply be in the world for a while. A real pleasure in that.

People forget, though, the constant motion. A fortnight moored, then off again. We've got to know the city's murky green veins so well, seen places we never knew existed. But in the dead of winter, as I wake by the necropolis under the looming gas towers of Kensal Green and realise, again, that work that week is out Tottenham way, it's no picnic. It's like anything. Ups and downs, right?

My mother thinks this is all one giant mistake. She can't understand *why* people can't afford bricks and mortar in which to live. Tom works, and so do I, but we don't earn enough. Not enough to live properly in this city. I'll choke myself in the weeds of the Lea before I surrender my wage to a uPVC nightmare, to junkspace new-builds built on the rubble of libraries. None of this computes with my mum. We must be lazy, inept, frivolous. She thinks marriage would somehow be a salve to what she sees as our problems. She spouts platitudes about the problem of young people today, only we're not getting any younger.

A decision had to be made. We took, like many, to the water. Not quite necessity, but not exactly choice. Tom fancied himself as a man with a practical bone in him, but he and I were, at first, a fucking shambles. I laugh to think of when we first got on *Peg*, the boat pitching to the right and left in damp April rain as two grizzled canal-folk watched, grinning, as we tried to move in. Try lugging all your gear through a door straight out of *Alice in Wonderland*, in Converse shoes that slip on damp wood with the realisation that water isn't as solid as earth and that this place that was going to become our home *moved*. Tom banged his head hard, a splinter sticking out of angry red skin.

'Lisa, for fuck's sake, stop laughing,' Tom shouted. But I had to. Cooped up for so long in the rabbit hutches of the renters, no stake in any place we lived, we didn't have a clue on how to *do* anything. I could barely tie a knot. The last time I'd painted a wall or, in fact, done anything practical beyond cooking and giving work-surfaces a wipe, was when I lived at home with my parents. The parents who bought their home for something like thirty grand back in the day. You know, when people with an unassuming job could afford to live in London. Words like 'generator', 'motor' and 'moorings' were opaque to me, from a lexicon that was other people's business.

Now even the canals that have become home are becoming cramped, competition for space increasing almost monthly. Problems have a tendency to replicate themselves.

But we can't leave the city, it's our home. I won't do it, not yet. I won't abandon it to the Eton set and Russian gangsters, to the oil sheikhs and people with *portfolios*.

Being here on *Peg*, I am reminded constantly of my grandad, drowned in the eighties, a stupid boating accident out on the Thames near Gravesend. He was not an old man. I find it hard to push away thoughts of grasping algaed hands gripping ankles tight; tendrilled water plants choking and grasping, the colour of regurgitated spinach. It all seemed like such a waste.

I know I'm lucky compared to so many other countless millions who crowd the surface of the earth, but even here bobbing by Markfield Park with the swifts screaming around my ears and greylag geese poking their heads up above the reservoir's parapet, life can feel like such a slog. Constant thoughts of where to move next. Worry about work. Unstable or freelance work gets you stuck in the present tense. Then there's those deeper worries that the day-to-day stress pushes down, and in that pushing down to focus my own stupid shit, guilt builds, knowing that I am trapped in this system, even nestled within *Peg*. I don't have it that bad, not by a long way. But I notice things. I'm seeing fewer birds in the skies – I *know* I am, I must trust my memories or everything falls apart. I'm seeing the boats multiply and jostle around us, watching old Nell sit on her bench by Markfield slurping down that corrosive booze. I can feel the seams of the city stretching. I smell exhaust in the air. I see a skyline become cluttered with buildings no one, surely, could want. There are too many of us. It's as simple as that.

You make a life-changing decision, feel that burst of elation, then wake up the next day to a beeping phone realising work never ends, teaching the same bored and restless kids their proper nouns and prepositions. Having watched one round of the seasons, down here on the city's waters, progress seems illusory and the spiral, the merry-go-round, is all there is.

*

I sit out on *Peg*'s deck, sipping scalding coffee that steams like a witch's brew in the cool of the morning. I feel the slightest bob of the water as I stare up at the gas tower, looming above our mooring like the stripped skeleton of a coliseum. They look unfinished and I do not know how they work. It was five years in London before I even possessed the words to describe them. Saw them from the windows of chugging trains, the occasional walk along the waterways with Tom when the weather was right, but I never really saw them. Now I have more time to notice. Now I have pinned some meaning to them. Unfinished sentry towers for the would-be guardians of the waters.

Mist hangs above the water, will-o'-the-wisp clumps already melting in the sun. We're here for two weeks. Close to the Ladbroke Grove Sainsbury's, absurd how its clean world of beeping tills and 2-for-1s juts right onto the towpath. Useful though; we need to eat, after all.

I hear a heavy splash somewhere out in the mist. Kids throwing stuff, perhaps a diving cormorant, the take-off of a swan or goose. I daydream that it's an otter, an escaped European beaver, even a hated mink.

A man in too-short shorts and a tight black T-shirt jogs along the towpath, huffing ostentatiously, eyes locked on the middle-distance. White wires plunge from his ears into a device strapped to his waist. He drops suddenly, pumps himself up and down in a series of assured push-ups. The lives of the healthy make me smile. Back on his feet, he jogs off in the direction of Wormwood Scrubs.

Tom pops his head up from somewhere below deck. He's wearing a misshapen jumper the colour of the canal.

'Morning love.' He squints, heavy eyes adjusting to the new day.

I hear the heavy splash again. This proximity to life.

'You not working today?' he asks with a half-yawn.

'Not today. The job fell through. Back to the search.'

'Sorry babe. We'll be alright.'

I say nothing. I can't bear these stock sayings, this padding in our language. Tom's breath leaks, ghostly in the chill of the morning. What am I to say? That everything will be OK?

'I've gotta go get ready,' he says finally, and disappears.

*

I think of the city's layers. What lies beneath. The canals, just one of many apt metaphors for the city, my city. Since I've lived here, the stories of the waters have started to grip harder and tighter. I hunt down books and articles about the lore of the Lea, the ghosts of the Grand Union. In the Oxfam bookstore in Angel, digging through paperbacks, I found a copy of C.L. Nolan's collection *Mucklebones*. Written in 1912, but decked out in one of those lurid seventies covers, a cheap reprint with a bootleg feel. 'Happy Birthday Jimmy!' was written in faded biro on the inside cover. The cover depicted a grinning green hag rising from stagnant and scummy water with grasping, outstretched hands. Hair like rotten duckweed, mossy teeth.

On Abebooks I tracked down a guidebook published in the late '80s by the defunct Malachite Press. *Spectres of the Towpath: The Folklore of Britain's Waterways*. Tales of the phantom fishermen and white foxes of the Swale in Kent. The festering Weychester and Blackmore canal in Hookland. The skinned and headless bears found floating in the River Lea, back around the time of the IRA hunger strikers. The dead of Kensal Green Cemetery shuffling along the towpath beneath the gas towers. These waters, so full of life, are correspondingly flooded with death.

My small pile of books is placed in a spot inside *Peg*, aimed to avoid any chance of the damp seeping in. Though perhaps it would be appropriate.

*

Greasy summer rain drips down *Peg*'s windows. I'm inside, curled up on a beanbag reading *Mucklebones*. Tom is out at work. In 'The Weed' Nolan writes: *'Green tendrils beckoned from below the scum of the cut; he had one option. Submersion.'*

I flick idly through the other stories. 'Ginny'. 'The Heron'. 'Flood Drain'. I can't help but think of those seventies public information films voiced by Donald Pleasence, English children dying in creative ways as a warning to us, the lucky: stay away from the dark and lonely water.

Nolan had it right. That's London life: sink or swim.

*

We've been arguing about money. Piloting *Peg* through the city, passing blocks of flats half-built that reach into the heavens, hearing the screech of green parakeets. Signage and boarded up patches of empty space recently acquired for development. My teaching work is still intermittent, never enough. But I try to save what little we have. Things can change, I'm applying for steady work whenever I can. That was the whole point of moving onto the waters, to save a little, to put something aside. To not have to live the life of the renters. But whatever we have just leaks away.

Tom earns more regularly than me but maybe Mum is right. He blows it, drinking it down the pub with his mates, snorting it up his nose at weekends. Smoking hash with PK and talking impossible politics while they sit by *Peg* and *Ginny*, passing judgement on the passers-by. If I can't picture a future, then Tom's given up trying.

So we argue. I hate myself when we do it, my voice sounding shrill, unpleasant, the shriek of a coot. I become the nag I never wanted to be. He pushes me into that role and I hate him for it. There's no space. It's just the two of us in cramped conditions, too much time together and in too-close proximity.

I'm going under.

*

We're moored up by Markfield Park again. The sun has dimmed.

Blackness is starting to colonise the water.

Tom is out, drinking at The Anchor & Hope with PK and I don't care when he comes back.

A muted splash, somewhere out there.

I sit silently inside of *Peg*, malfunctioning dongle shoved into a laptop orifice, watching websites I don't really want to look at buffer endlessly. Then there's a knock at the window, and I see Jess's smiling face at the window. I'm glad she's here and invite her in. There's the nagging sense we're the ones left behind while the men talk and drink, even though I was half-heartedly invited. The so-called alternative lifestyles we lead.

Jess hands me a cold cider, I crack the can open, we say cheers and she settles down on the small sofa. I'm sprawled out on my beanbag, feeling suddenly sullen and childish.

'You alright Lisa?'

And I want to tell her how nothing ever works out the way you'd imagine it and how I feel that the freedom of the water in my city has only brought different problems. How I feel I'm drowning in London, how there's never enough work and enough money, or when I do have the work I resent it and wish I was back on the boat. How I feel claustrophobic now with Tom, too close all the time, how at night I dream of my grandfather being dragged down by watery women below the grey waters of the Thames. How I feel glad in a strange way that he never saw the new build flats and the demolished libraries and a franchise coffee outlet on every corner. How I envy the swifts above the reservoir and the glorious arcs of their wings that take them all the way to Africa. How at times I even envy Nell on her bench with her gutrot cider and a black dog sniffling among the discarded crisp packets.

I say, 'Yeah not too bad.'

*

I haven't had any work in two weeks. Stuck on the boat, just books to read and a radio that only imparts bad news for company.

Autumn has come. Chill in the air. The swifts have gone.

Tom is out at work. I didn't even bother getting out of bed to kiss him goodbye. He'll only be back again later. I want to leap off the boat and begin running, like all those joggers I see every day, just keep running and running until the canals run out and I have nowhere left to go.

Outside it's misty, and drizzle patters my skin as I emerge from *Peg* to look at the navigation. I roll a cigarette and blow smoke clouds into the mist.

I decide to take a walk, up to Tottenham Lock, maybe a bit further, just stretch the legs and get myself calibrated for the day. Too much time spent curled like a cat on that dirty beanbag, reading *Mucklebones* and waiting for the internet to work.

So I walk, passing buggy-pushing Hasidic women, a young man shouting angrily down his phone as he looks over the water, dog walkers, other boaters like myself, glimpsed furtively through dirty glass. Nell sits on a bench by the bridge, motionless, and I think I should say hello or attempt some form of contact but I do not.

At the Lock things are still, hushed. Industrial warehouses crowd the bank opposite. I stand at the water's edge, looking down into water where green plants sway slowly. I hear a laugh, a cracked chuckle, mirthless, malicious. I think of mossy and algaed claws, clutching and never letting go.

There is one choice in this city. Submersion.

VI.
Up and Coming

Nights like this. That's what it's all about. On my own, somewhere out there in the real world, I don't feel like I add up to much. Too much don't make sense. There's this sense of just keeping my head above water, sometimes even fucking drowning. But here I float.

Tonight's the last night I'll ever stand here doing this. Last night at The Stockwell Arms before all change; *this service terminates here*. The décor, the demographic, the price of the beer, everything. I feel uneasy to be feeling this moment, right now, right here in the present, knowing that when I wake tomorrow with the inevitable hangover it'll be the past, already a memory, a place we talk about fondly in the past tense until even the stories fade and distort.

The crowd's even more wild and unruly than usual, which isn't surprising. No one is getting barred tonight. I'm standing at the bar chatting with Canadian Dave, Simon and his missus

Ade, and some mate of theirs from Bristol, Jess. She's a bit younger than us, in her twenties by the looks.

I get a sense of communion from these nights, a shared feeling and commonality that can be embarrassing when first encountered. The first time I found this, and I'm not ashamed to say it, I felt this surge inside like I was going to cry or something. A long time ago now that was. It was the first time things made any fucking sense to me. A place where I didn't feel alone. A place I didn't want to leave. Trust me on this one, it was beautiful.

I'm waiting for the barmaid to appear. I tap a beer mat on the bar as I look around. The men and women here, whose ages straddle generations (and here that's OK, it really is), they're all here for a reason. That reason, if not quite the same for each and all, overlaps, intersects and intertwines. The older men and women, pushing well into their thirties, believe they've seen it all before and are eager to let everyone know; they've seen a lot, sure, their tats are starting to fade and blur a little, but I reckon they've still got a thing or two to learn. I should know: I am one of them.

Then there's ones even older, pushing or jumping clean over the half-century, the ones who can remember 'Do They Owe Us A Living' first time round, the ones who can talk about free festivals that really were free and a world that sounds less codified. Some of them are arrogant pricks to be honest, reminding you that they were here first and don't you forget it son. But most of them are decent people, in it for life, and there's this sense of continuity I get when I speak to them that I love. I think of myself twenty thirty years down the line telling wide-eyed young ones about the old bloke *I knew* who'd seen Crass first hand. *No way*, I imagine they'll say. Maybe they won't give a shit though. For the decent ones, time's softened their arrogance, mainly, but the booze has taken its toll on a significant minority. It's true, there's no denying it. It's a risk we all run. I put my hands up,

I'm as bad as any of them at times. Pint in hand on a splintery pub table in the English summer sun, just before a gig kicks off inside, that's fucking heaven to me. As I've gotten older it's only become more true.

Then of course there's the younger ones, like Jess, showing off the fresh tattoos for all to see, skin still red and sore, their jackets maybe a bit too clean, badges pinned and patches sewn all over. The new Doc Martens buffed to within an inch of their life. I did all that myself, of course I did. I always veered towards the skin side of the whole punk thing, and took a lot of pride in the way I'd turn myself out on gig nights, jeans clean and well-fitting, boots shined and making me feel ten-foot-tall, Harrington over a tight black T-shirt with an anarcho band across the front, or if I was going proper smart, then a navy or crimson Fred Perry buttoned up to the neck. It was like the uniform of my real life; jokingly I called the gear I wore to work, or when I went to go and see me mum and dad, me civvies. I guess I had a point to prove, to myself more than anyone, and in those clothes I felt like *me*. When you find something in this world – which, let's be honest, can be pretty fucking miserable a lot of the time – that actually means a damn thing, you cling on for dear life. You commit to it. There's a dignity to that, there really is.

I know a lot of folks who think it's juvenile. That's something that gets me. Really niggles, you know? If your overriding passion in life is paintings or books or films or fishing or even the fucking footy then it's alright to be into that, with a blinding passion, for your whole life. With music (not the classical shite) it's different somehow. A young man and woman's game, the world reckons. I've still never got me head fully round that one. Less booze and drugs and fights at the galleries and the poetry readings I guess; but then I've met a lot of poets and writers, and let me tell you they can cane it and drink up there with the best of them. Saw some of them go down k-holes they could never climb back out of, or become cocaine cunts nobody could bear to be around, or believed all that shite about Dylan Thomas and Bukowski and the rest of the drinkers with a writing problem. Sad really. The song said ignorance was the British disease (a cracking song, no lie), but trust me, it's the pints and powder.

The young ones have the look and thrill of recent converts. I envy them that; you can't ever get it back. Not all of them will go the distance of course. They've got a good decade of guilt-free enjoyment before they've gotta start thinking do they really like this? And is this any way for an adult, someone in their thirties forties fifties to behave? That's a choice they've yet to make and it's an enviable position. They're the ones who'll buy the copies of *Magnesium Burns* and *Frontline* and *Punk Positive* and read them cover-to-cover. The ones who don't seem to quite believe that me and my mates were there up at The Balustrade before the bastards sold the place, before the developers were let in. The developers who turned it into flats and a fucking Costa Coffee. I swear the council were nobbled.

It's something I'm seeing more and more as I get older. I feel a responsibility to remember these things. Like if I don't remember and dig out the photos and say, yeah I was there and it was like this, then it may as well never have happened. When I went down to see Simon and Ade a few weeks back, down in Kent, he dug out a load of pics of all of us up at The Balustrade. Good times. All of us thinner and with sillier haircuts. One pic was creased in this way that split Ade from head to navel – it's an image I can't get out my head for some reason. It was on Balustrade Street, in case you're wondering about the name.

Finally, the barmaid appears with a sweaty smile and she's either overworked, pissed or taken something, but whatever, it's fine. Tonight's the last night and no one cares. I order a round of drinks, ciders for the lot of us, passing the glasses over a sea of people to Simon who takes them to the table we've managed to secure. I hand Canadian Dave his pint and he nods seriously in thanks. I fight my way out of the scrum at bar, a bit of cider slopping over me. I hiss in annoyance.

*

The gigs, the London ones at least, they all seem to be getting pushed further and further out. I can talk of a time when all this stuff happened in Hackney and Brixton, even Islington for chrissakes, but now I find myself standing in venues in Tottenham or Deptford or bloody Tufnell Park where it's impossible to get to when the Northern Line goes down, which it always does. It's not right. Now even Deptford's getting tarred with the *up-and-coming* brush. How the hell did that happen?! When I'm feeling paranoid, I call it social cleansing by stealth. Maybe that's a bit much, but there's something in it. And it's not even that stealthy. It's brazen.

When I see punks spark-out on dirty mattresses, pissing up against the walls of venues or openly drinking their shop-bought cans, I want to slap them. There's a group of them outside now on the wall, slurping down Scrumpy Jack and smoking superkings. I want to shake some sense into them.

This modern blankness seeps into everything. This nihilism. Life became much harder and at the same time a belief in anything better became a kind of embarrassment. Get back to the eighties John where you belong, my mates and family laugh. They're going too far back anyway; I came up in the nineties. In '89 I was only twelve years old. Spiritually though, Susie said, you belong somewhere around 1984. It was probably true and contributed to the breakup, no doubt about it. I'm no good at this constant erasure and daily amnesia. I need a timeline. I need to know history didn't end. So, less Pistols, more One Way System. Give us a future and all that.

*

I squeeze into the booth next to Jess, Canadian Dave opposite, Simon and Ade wedged into a corner.

You better not need a piss for the next twenty minutes, I say to them. They laugh.

I pull out my baccy tin, set it down on the cider-sticky table. Before I've even started rolling, Jess pipes up and asks, 'Can I nick a fag off you?'

'Course you can.'

'Nice one.'

We push through the crowd outside, into the small patch of concrete that passes as the outdoor drinking area and onto the pavement in front of the pub. The group necking their tins of Scrumpy Jack are still sat on the wall. Some of them will be out here all night, won't even bother paying to come into the gig. It irritates me.

'Never been to this venue before,' Jess says in her Bristol accent.

'Your timing's impeccable,' I say, and light our cigarettes.

I exhale a cloud of blue smoke. As I do a woman passes me, pushing a buggy. I recognise her; my neighbour Lucy.

'Alright Lucy,' I say.

'Oh, hello John. I didn't know you came here?'

'All the time. Last night tonight. Shame.'

'Well good to see you, I've got to dash, this little one has been keeping me busy, you know.' She smiles a tired smile.

I look at the sleeping child. Lucy looks awkward, scans the crowd of drunks and black jackets.

'See you soon,' I say.

*

Sometimes I look in the mirror in the morning for longer than is strictly necessary. John Whitefield, born 1977, one failed marriage, no kids, greying stubble, keeping my hair at a respectable length. I don't go full skin these days. People will just think I'm another white bloke going bald, or worse, a fucking Nazi. Ten years I've lived round here, and nearly everything I loved about the place has gone. I've changed too, I know that, but The Stockwell Arms going feels like the end of something. I find myself entertaining fantasies of leaving the city for good. Woods and hills and rivers and that. At times I find myself even tiring of my own interests, and that's a dreadful thing. Punk to me meant at least some kind of ideology, a belief in something, not this creeping nihilism I see around me. The world feels like it's knackered and in a post-ideological freefall.

I'm not saying this is entirely a new thing. There was always an aspect of that; the chaos punks who believed all the no future crap and could only see as far ahead as their next drink. I read a book about this kind of thing recently. Depressed hedonism was the term. I'm seeing a lot of depressed hedonists these days; and not just the punks and skins (we're so few after all). If I head up the Kingsland Road on a Friday night there's hundreds of them out and about, kids and even proper grownups with their knocked-together looks, hotch-potch aesthetics grave-robbed from subcultures that once meant something. Including *my* culture. If I see one more Black Flag T-shirt I think my head's going to explode.

Not that I head up Kingsland Road much these days. I don't have anything against hipsters really, and I tend not to cross paths with many of them on a day-to-day basis. But they look lost to me. Oddly, I feel like they've given up. Like they've seen the future and know it's boring and pointless. I follow something of a uniform, I know that – but I never said I was an individual.

I think about how we all just inhabit roles that exist without us. Like when I was a snotty teen punk-skin I was *me*, sure, but I also fitted into a role and someone else's idea of what that thing should be, and I saw others that way too. We all talk about individuality, about how it's the thing to aim for and the thing to be celebrated and so on. But if I'm honest I think that's bollocks. Where does it leave family for a start? And we all want to belong. Be a part of something. I'm happy to say I'm me, but I'm also a part of this thing that's bigger than me and I feed it and it feeds me. And beyond this little sub-culture then I'm a part of my street, the city I live in, part of the country, part of the whole world. I'm sounding like a hippy now, but it's true.

A lot of the pigshit-thick skins and the crusty punks out of their heads on whatever internet powder is flavour of the week, they don't think in these terms. I've met my fair share of narcissists over the years, trust me. But I've thought about this issue long and hard as I've got older, and the stuff I thought I'd grow out of just didn't fade away. I don't feel like I'm immature; but is that assessment one only others can make? There I go again, trying to be the bar room philosopher, just like Frankie Stubbs.

The young punks and skins have modern technology on their side. Now on that one, I'm not sure I envy them. It seems counter-intuitive, I know, but I think they've gained something but lost a lot fucking more. Maybe this is just the grumbling of an older man. Like every old git, ever, has spouted. In the early days of the scene, it's true, tracking down this music and knowing this history was a challenge. Even when I was young it was difficult, but we always found a way and maybe that's the point. This ease of access, this clear difference between the three generations, it's a problem at times. All people, in all cultures, everywhere, are expected to earn their stripes somehow and in this sense of discovering the culture, younger people do have it easier. But, still, it always comes back to the unanswerable question just what it is that makes a person like *this* and not *that* and the whole beautiful mystery of sub-culture is forever up for debate. And I could have done with eBay and YouTube and Spotify when I was young; the music I can get now blows my mind. It makes me think about what person I would've been had I had all this stuff when I was a nipper; would I have been happier, more broad-minded, or exactly the same? Remembering those pre-internet days makes me already feel like something of a relic. There'll come a time when there's no one alive who will know a world without it. Now there's a thought.

*

We're back at the table sipping cider.

You can guess what's happening to The Stockwell Arms. Someone made the owner an offer that was too good to refuse. It must be way past the million mark for a gaffe like this one. Frankly I'd take the money and run too. Who wouldn't? This is real life we're talking about. But it's a crying shame because I knew what would happen to the place, I just knew it. Canadian Dave is telling the table how the whole place is getting gastro'd with a few luxury flats above.

'Sign of the times, man,' he says, 'sign of the times,' and fiddles with his black cap. Always turned out head to toe in black is Canadian Dave, usually with some tee that's more metal than punk. I almost laugh, and I say, 'I told you this would happen.' But there's no joy in being right.

'It's a real shame,' says Jess, looking thoughtfully into her drink.

'You lot should move to Kent,' says Simon. I'm telling you. London's over.

'Shut up Simon,' says Ade and lightly slaps his face.

'Shall we go in?' I ask, draining my pint.

Gary Budden

VII.
Knotweed

The cat killed a bird this morning. A fledgling chaffinch, its right-hand side shredded open and oozing thick liquid, a few matted feathers stuck to the exposed meat. I got it off him, his amber eyes surprised at the intrusion. The bird died a few minutes later, its heart giving up, the shock too much. I couldn't bear giving it back to the cat so I buried it near the potato patch. I felt nauseous as I lay the tiny body to rest under the dark earth.

I wish I could explain to him not to murder the bees, the few sparrows and starlings that come to this patch of grass in north west London. They're dying. It isn't his fault, I know, it's mine, ours, somebody's. Dan says we're the only species capable of realising, and therefore changing, our instincts.

Dan had left for work an hour before. I sat at the kitchen table drinking black coffee, thinking of a tiny body hatched only days earlier. The cat purred and rubbed himself against my legs. I kicked him away.

I set out to meet Sofia, warm June drizzle in the air as I walked to the station. I sat on the brick wall at West Hampstead Overground. Eight minutes until the train. A few other commuters were spread out across the platform, staring at the tracks. Drizzle spotted my cheeks. My jacket was stifling in the unexpected humidity. I rubbed my stomach and thought something moved. Too lethargic to listen to music or read my novel, I let the rain fall. Behind the opposite platform, dug out of the railway embankment, was a patch of exposed earth, fenced off with a metal sign:

CONTAMINATED SOIL DO NOT DISTURB THIS AREA IS BEING TREATED FOR JAPANESE KNOTWEED.

A grey squirrel stop-started over the infected earth before bounding into the mesh of bindweed, Special Brew cans, bramble, willowherb, faded crisp packets and buddleia. Three green parakeets screeched overhead.

I was on my way to meet Sofia in the north east of the city. She and my other London friends didn't understand why, when I'd finally elected to return after my five-year stint on the Kent coast, I hadn't rejoined them in the crowded cafes and hangovers of Dalston and Hackney Downs. The memories were tiring. I wanted to raise children in the metropolis, not in the salt sadness of Margate. But the Hackney of my twenties was exhausting.

'Helena,' they said, 'why the hell would you want to live all the way out there? Kilburn may as well as be the moon. There's nothing to *do* out there.' People laughed, I smiled politely, wanting to explain all the things they couldn't understand and I could not say.

It takes twenty-two minutes from West Hampstead to Dalston Kingsland. I live close by. It's no cheaper out this way, but Dan and I managed to get a half-decent flat with an actual garden. I'm doing my best to reacquaint myself with the names of plants; things I was good at as a child. I enjoy the names of herbs and wildflowers that grow on the unloved railway embankments, a different lexicon for understanding the city. Speaking their names aloud feels like an antidote to something, a palate cleanser.

My time living on the coast, we had more space and a garden that was only ever half-tended, stocked with local art, carved driftwood terns and ceramic selkies, and a metal thing that hung from a tree, tinny in the breeze. The sea, the salt and shingle, was the draw down there. Gulls, cheap rent, space to work, melancholia. In the end, Dan said he missed the busyness of the city, and I agreed. Said I wanted to do it on our terms though. We weren't in our twenties anymore, can't go back to the 4am Thursday nights, white lines on cut mirror-glass.

'My mum used to live around Dollis Hill way, before I was born. I always quite liked it round there,' Dan said. 'It's on the Overground.'

'Let's look then,' I said.

A year later, we were back in the comforting anonymity of the city, with a new postcode to match a new perspective. It bothers me people didn't understand.

I stared at the information board. Five minutes to the train. That dead chaffinch, small, buried with the potatoes. I hoped nothing would disturb it, that it was left in peace. Feeling my stomach, I gazed at the sign.

Japanese knotweed. I'd read about it an article in *Ham&High* someone left on the tube. The plant was everywhere, invading the homes of the famous; an absurdly wealthy footballer up in Hampstead; TV celebrities we thought had been left stranded in the nineties. They said it can grow ten centimetres a day, roots that punch through concrete, brick, wooden floors. Tenacious like bamboo and as aggressive as a triffid, it could knock tens of thousands off property prices: a plant unconcerned by aspirational lifestyles, disrespectful to the English landscape garden, uncaring of hopes sunk in bricks and mortar. It could ruin this station. It is a beautiful plant.

I sat on the wall in the rain. An overgrown and ruined London. Barclays and Costa Coffee overtaken, submerged and redundant. Starbucks and Topshop abandoned like the temples I saw at Angkor Wat, on the first trip we ever took abroad as a couple. Left for our survivors. Families of rust-furred foxes padding through the knotweed jungles, grey squirrels skittering through the trees, packs of cats hunting them as parakeet flocks scream overhead. Escaped animals from London Zoo adapting to a defunct metropolis. A leopard padding through the overgrowth hunting fallow deer. Muntjac picking their way through grassy streets. A few feral humans, dealing in ruined paperbacks, salvaged clothing and the detritus of a culture long gone. Happy daydreams.

My phone vibrated somewhere deep within my bag. A text from Dan: *they've fenced off part of West Hampstead, the triffids are taking over, have a look when you get there!! Have a great day babe, say hi to Sof from me xx.*

I looked around, saw at least fifteen other people, old and young, mirroring my actions. Eyes locked onto a small screen, thumbing words. I felt ashamed, just another part of the London crowd. I didn't text Dan back.

I like where I live. I wish I could explain better. I walk to places like Roundwood Park on the Harlesden-Willesden border, where I often climb the small hill and look out over the city to Wembley stadium, rearing out of the sprawl like a breaching whale, across over the sombre Jewish cemetery, at pink-brown jays, snogging teens, buggy pushers. It's not the city I knew and I like that. I was done with the coast, had exhausted that salty fugue state just in time to jump ship before it became fashionable. Once again. I had friends, now, who were looking at Victorian houses in Margate, Ramsgate, Broadstairs. They didn't like it, but god it was *cheap*. The Victorians brought the knotweed to these shores as ornamental garden decoration.

Pests, weeds, these terms are subjective.

The train was crowded and sweaty. I stood and stared out the window as the contaminated patch of earth faded from view, wondering what chemicals were being put down. Surely they were worse than the knotweed? Twenty-two minutes later and I was in Hackney, pushing out onto Kingsland Road as if I still owned the streets like I once had and, yeah, I felt a pang when I thought back seven, eight, nine years when I'd stood on that very patch of pavement *there* smoking the rollies I have finally managed to quit, walking that first time hand-in-hand with Dan and crackling with energy. Whoever thought we'd still be together best part of a decade later? So much has happened in what seems like a blink, but we all say that don't we? This mix of the two of us, that's why I'm thinking like this. I haven't told anyone. Not yet. What will the city, this part of town, be like when my child is thirty-two, when I am sixty-four? Will Margate have sunk under the grey waves? Will Hampstead be a knotweed forest? Will the foxes take over? What shape will the world take? Will our children stand on these streets and drink and smoke and laugh as we did? I hope so.

I passed the market, the smell of fish entrails triggering my nausea once again. The refurbished bar where I once worked (I was a terrible pint-puller). I don't regret these memories and neither do I want them back. I texted Dan. He doesn't know yet. I wanted to tell him that night, in person.

The afternoon passed with milky coffee, a toasted sandwich for Sofia who today seemed bony and girlish. I was less queasy now so I ordered Turkish menemen.

'Aren't you a vegan anymore?' she asked.

'Just your usual run-of-the-mill vegetarian these days.'

I haven't been a vegan for nearly four years. She remembers me as I was.

We talked, sharing stories and gossip about friends past and present, giggling at events from half a decade ago, news that Dave and Lucy are engaged with a baby on the way (the perfect moment to drop my news, but I held back). We wondered whatever happened to Chris, retold the story of how Deb found love with an Aussie and moved out to Melbourne.

Sofia started to talk about new art exhibitions opening near the market, of new films and recently published novels, but I started talking house prices and my plans for the future. Sofia glazed over, but I continued, bringing up the knotweed, the facts I'd read in the paper, the Victorians who brought it here as an ornamental plant, the beauty that got way out of control, how it can devalue a house by £250,000.

'Why are you going on about knotweed?'

'I don't know. It's interesting, that's all.'

Sofia smiled weakly. She knows the knotweed could never affect her world of flats and cafes, of art and nicotine. I let her take the reins of the conversation. I talked little about Kilburn. She talked about folk I half-remember who loom large in her life, events going on in the next few weeks that I should attend, if traveling back is a problem then I can always stay at hers. I nodded and made promises we both know I'll break. I didn't tell her my news. I don't want that conversation, not yet, and anyway not with her. Sofia looked hungover, sunken eyes in a child's face, and I felt a ripple of pity, then guilt, at judging her.

A moment of silence, then I said, 'Come on, show me what's changed around here then.'

We nosed through vintage shops where I wondered what we'll consider vintage in thirty-two years. We took periodic coffee stops, rummaged through creased paperbacks in Oxfam. I said no to the pub at the end of it all and headed back to the station feeling like a grownup.

Evening by the time I got back to West Hampstead station. No one to be seen working on the infected earth. I decided to walk the distance home. The day's early rain had drained off the humidity. It was a nice night and I enjoyed the hum of the street. I passed young couples holding hands, heard the bark of foxes starting their day and saluted a drunk who wished me Merry Christmas despite it being June. This city.

Home, the cat greeted me cheerfully. An aroma of cumin and coriander leaked from the kitchen. Dan was in there doing vegetable curry. I entered and kissed him on the cheek.

'Hello love. How was your day? Did you get my text?'

'Yeah I did. Didn't see what you were talking about though, I was rushing for the train.' I lied. The knotweed forests are for me and me alone.

'Look it up, crazy stuff. Anyway, what did you want to tell me? Some news or something?'

My husband's face was shrouded in steam rising from the curry pot. Thick smells in the air. He wiped his damp forehead and stirred the pot.

'Oh, nothing much. Can't remember now.'

Gary Budden

VIII.
Shell Grottoes

Remember the grotter.

That's what they used to say.

Shingle crunches under the vampire hunter's feet. He watches flickering twists of flame light up homes of oystershell, miniature cairns made by young people that illuminate this shore during the festival.

He doesn't know if he remembers the words from life, from one of his many books or if he's channeling it from somewhere else entirely (when did he first visit this town at the mouth of the estuary?). He's old and he can remember the grotters. He will check the reference at home. It's in one of his books, he is sure.

Tomorrow, his friend of a lifetime, the vampire, will be visiting him here at the estuary's mouth, for the festival that gives thanks to the waters that give the town its life. It's a yearly tradition they maintain in their old age.

The young construct the grottoes, even now, from the shell of the creature that made this town famous. Swimming in its own liquor, a genuine taste of the sea sucked from rough shell.

They were harvested as far back as Roman times, or so everyone says; a culture attributed with a great deal around here; the dock leaves and nettles growing in convenient proximity, the spit of mysterious shingle that juts out to sea from the town's beach, infant sacrifice at the garrison twelve miles away. So why not seafood cultivars? Perhaps if people wish it to be true, then it should be.

The vampire hunter knows it's easy to project onto the long dead and how tempting it can be. He knows the all-consuming power of fiction, what the stories he helped create mean and how they consumed him also.

He has added a genteel celebrity to the town and has enjoyed a long and varied life. The vampire hunter is the politest man you will ever meet; he has lived a life of horror. He has seen things, more than most.

Watching the fires that writhe like trapped elementals, he recalls some of his past lives:

Leading a fearsome band on the Romney Marshes, smuggling rum and tobacco through waterlogged reeds, fighting the king's men not too far from the town that became his home.

Aeons spent as a scientist lacking in moral fibre – he could breathe life where none should be.

A time-travelling and ageless being, but even that couldn't last. New faces always appear. The only constant was change, he knew now.

An Egyptologist among golden sands, disturbing the rest of the long dead.

The island's most famous detective, pipe in mouth, coolly analytical. (He was always a learned man, if not a decent one.)

The vampire hunter is stitched into the fabric of this island's story; he can feel himself coming to the end of his own limited perspective before he fuses, willingly, with that bigger thing, the ongoing story with one eternal narrator, or many, depending on your point of view. He knows that he will have an afterlife afforded only to the few and he used to wonder if he deserved such a thing. But age has taught him that no one gets what they deserve, not really, and that the concept itself is a strange one. Anyway, he'll be remembered not for what he was, but for what he pretended to be.

He has helped the island and its inhabitants find some form of escape, aided them in the struggle to face down their fears and allowed them to enjoy lurid entertainment splashed with poster-paint blood. We all yearn for the monstrous and the weird even as we shun it.

What monsters has the vampire hunter fought? Brucolacs, goatsuckers, the blood-hungry, sure. But to this list we must add other things: the animated remains of a body embalmed and bandage-wrapped. A stitched-together monstrosity of his own making. He recalls the huge snowy ape-thing that beleaguered him in the impossible mountains of the Himalayas, a snake-haired woman with a stony stare, and the eternal being thawed from ice that derailed the Trans-Siberian. He remembers them all so fondly, the lost friends to whom he will toast with the vampire tomorrow, as they always do.

The vampire hunter makes his slow way home, away from the festival and along the coast, past the Harbour Lights pub where men in leather jackets and women in short skirts smoke and drink, butts piling up by the wooden bench legs. One man, voice loose with drink and rough with tobacco, recognises him.

The man mimes a stake plunged into his heart, gasps, staggers back into the arms of the woman, moans, then laughs. His companions laugh also. The vampire hunter smiles, gives a small nod. This happens often.

His walk takes him back up the slopes where a rusted cannon on a concrete base stares blindly out to sea. The tide is retreating, exposing that mysterious shingle spit on which the vampire hunter himself has walked. Either side of the town stretch miles of saltmarsh, boggy ground where a few unwary lost themselves and never returned. The vampire hunter loves the marshes of his adopted hometown, unpeopled flatness where his mind can wander, a space waiting to be filled. It's known locally as the Hollow Shore, a name like the title of one of the vampire hunter's films. These echoes and suggestions please him greatly.

*

The vampire hunter was married, for decades. His wife was swiftly snuffed out by a disease more monstrous than any creature he had ever faced. It was after that that he found this town at the mouth of the estuary surrounded by saltmarsh and thought how, perhaps, he would trade in a life of horror and fear for one lulled by the sigh of the sea. He remembers telling his friend, the vampire, how they would never do battle again, but that he should, of course, visit him. Come for the festival, see the shell grottoes and the flickering flame.

*

Back at home, darkness falling rapidly, the vampire hunter brews tea and makes a simple supper. Remember the grotter?

He scans his bookshelves. That book there, it's familiar, jogs something inside of him. *Esoteric Kent: A Guide to the Hidden Walkways and Roads Less Travelled of the Garden of England*, published by the Malachite Press. This is an old edition, one he must have bought in the years just preceding his move to the town. He pulls it down, opens it and there it is, under the entry for the festival. He sees pencil marks made by his own hand, years back, underlining what he once thought important, and now does again.

The children... find a use for some [oyster shells] in the construction of grottoes, which they illuminate at night with a piece of candle, generally on the first of August. Probably few people remember the origin of the old street petition, 'Please remember the grotter!' The children who give utterance to it do so without reference to its appropriate day. The legend goes that a prominent holy man's remains were being returned from Palestine by boat. A knight charged with the remains' protection, and his horse, fell overboard. The knight was saved without his horse and, on being rescued, his clothes were found to be covered with clinging oysters. The miracle, associated with the presence of the holy, became the origin of the oyster grotto.

The vampire hunter cannot now help but think of how the forgotten rituals are some sort of armour against the monstrous realities of this world. Oystershell barricades to keep the dark at bay, a darkness given form in the very monsters that he fought, and in the main, defeated.

His interest is rekindled now. He takes down *Stories from the Marsh: The folklore of the Hollow Shore*. He takes it down, flicks through the pages. This copy is an original, very old; foreword penned by folklorist C.L. Nolan, a man long dead and largely forgotten. The vampire hunter recalls meeting an already-ancient Nolan when he was just a young man fighting his very first undead. Mooted talks to adapt the old-man's story 'The Sea Giant', that in the end came to nothing.

It's been a long time since he delved into the lore of his home. Each tale in the book is accompanied by a beautiful and melancholy woodcut. Birds feature heavily, with ghostly bittern, mournful curlews and majestic harriers. He lands on one story that feels deeply familiar, 'The White Heron'. A real species? The vampire hunter is unsure.

'Fear the shades of the reeds. White things that were lost to us, now returned.'

The author is simply marked anon.

*

The morning finds the vampire hunter at his desk, flicking through entries in both *Esoteric Kent* and *Stories from the Marsh*. He searches for more information concerning the festival, what it means, and if in fact there is any solid reality other than these half-remembered fictions and symbolic acts that make up the life he has lived.

The doorbell rings.

The vampire is as tall and imposing as he ever was despite the advancing years. Dressed all in fuligin black, he speaks in a deep baritone and commands the presence of those around him. Here is my mortal enemy and dearest friend, thinks the vampire hunter.

They sit in the kitchen talking, before they head out of the town to walk the Hollow Shore, listening to the burble of curlews and keeping watch for the elusive white egrets that have been spotted in the area after a generation of absence.

They return to a town heavy with crowds, filling with revellers celebrating the festival. The people are drinking hard, laughing, enjoying the temporary freedom of it all. What meaning do they ascribe to it? There must be something.

The vampire and the vampire hunter make their way once more to the seafront, and see children building new cairns of oystershell, next to piles of candles awaiting ignition.

'Why do they persist?' asks the vampire, as he watches two pale children kneel in the shingle. 'If they have forgotten the grotter, the roots of their rituals, then why do they persist?'

'They wish to stave off the dark. Like all of us.'

The vampire nods and regards his friend, who stares out over the estuary as the fires are ignited and the pitch of the festival increases. He looms over the grottoes like a being from the age of fables, willing the dark away.

Gary Budden

IX.
Bent Branches

Pen Yr Allt

Two red kites, rust and charcoal colours, circle in slow laps above the valley, the Severn sparkling beneath. I sit on the damp grass that forms a barrier between our rented cottage and the tree line of the Pen Yr Allt woods, Helena dozing beside me. A generation ago the kites were nearly extinct. I watch their slow spiral and remember the times when my dad drove us deep into Wales to look for the dwindling raptors. We drove further west from where I now sit, my wife fanned out on the grass next to me, soaking up the sun. I swig from a bottle of pear cider and light a cigarette while Helena sleeps, watching the circling birds, enjoying the optimism they give me. Not all stories are set in stone. Trajectories can be changed. The river flows and I wonder if redemption is possible.

The world sits somewhere there over the Severn, past an ugly line of felled pines up on the hill, uprooted and harvested by the

Forestry Commission who periodically plant, grow, uproot and harvest in an endless cycle. These pine forests are near-birdless, hostile to life, they shift and can't be trusted. Cycle-paths and walkways change with the seasons.

Helena wakes and stretches. We spend another two hours idle, eating an improvised picnic, looking out over the valley, saying little and enjoying the quiet. Finally, we opt to explore the surroundings. I sluggishly pull on suitable footwear. Helena, better rested than me, bounds up the steep incline into the woods. This heat is so unexpected. I follow, up an unofficial but well-worn path into the trees.

The woods lack human noise, only the two of us to snap dry twigs and crunch through fallen leaves. Not quiet, but a different kind of noise. The undergrowth teems with midges, gnats, beetles, butterflies, bees. Birds chirrup, mating songs fill the air, woodpigeons coo. A flapping pink jay bursts out from his hiding place. Wood cracks beneath Helena's feet like the crack of gunshot. She bought new hiking boots, especially for this trip, last week in Brent Cross Shopping Centre. I remember the argument at the returns counter of one of those interchangeable clothing stores. A woman, trembling with rage and losing the argument she'd started, spat in her opponent's face. We stood and watched, did nothing. Don't get involved. Such things seem absurd today.

A huge Great Dane bounds out of the trees onto the path in front of us, one of the many spectral hounds that haunt all corners of the island, a ghost of Gelert. I flinch, stand back while Helena becomes visibly excited. The dog runs into her embrace like it's greeting a long-lost lover, she pats and rubs the giant animal, cooing a soothing 'hello girl' and 'look at you, you're lovely'. This dog is real, here and now, no beast from Celtic mythology. Cautiously I join my wife and stroke the thick bristling fur.

The owner appears, affable and friendly, four other plus-size hounds fanning out in front of him, his loyal vanguard. He's young, mid-twenties at most and the only soul we've seen in hours. I wonder what his life out here in quiet central Wales must be like. So different from a life defined by salt water and concrete. We make the required small talk, though I find myself enjoying it, Helena talking of how she desperately wants a dog but it's a lot of commitment, especially in London and it's not fair to keep them cooped up. The young man nods with genuine interest. I find myself agreeing with my wife. I fantasise about walking a husky on daily trips through Gladstone Park, letting curious children stop and pat him or her, scooping up mess and dumping it in a red bin. The troupe of hounds and their leader move on and we wave our goodbyes and nice-to-meet-yous.

My mind unfolds like a map when I have access to a horizon, can walk the woods and can see, not theorise, a river. I scratch one of three lumpy mosquito bites on my right hand.

We step into a clearing and see a red kite circling overhead, perhaps one of the pair I watched earlier. Muddy ruts from recent bicycle trips cut through the earth, the crusted ridges drying out and hardening in the sun to a light grey-brown. It's sweltering today, caught us off guard. We didn't pack the right gear, our minds on auto-pilot saying: rain, cold, take jumpers and waterproofs. Beads form on my forehead. Helena strides ahead.

Rituals

We woke early, too early for the tube. Anyway, we didn't want to share our journey with the previous night's party-casualties, their dilated eyes, tobacco stink and embarrassment too much a reflection of our younger selves.

We cabbed it to Euston. I regretted the couple of beers the night before, argued our set-piece *we're tired and irritable* argument that was forgotten by the time we hit the queue at Caffè Nero. A ceremonial observance, we knew the script off by heart, familiar and reassuring.

Helena sort-of-slept on the train, jerking awake at Rugby, bleary-eyed at Coventry. I watched the West Midlands through smeared glass, too tired to read but unable to sleep. I devoured an overpriced egg baguette during the twenty-minute change at Birmingham New Street.

'Waste of four pound fifty. You should have had breakfast,' Helena murmured and stroked her belly. She was right, of course. From Birmingham to Caersws she slept again as kids ran up and down the carriage, their accents a muddle of Liverpool, the Welsh borders, Black Country. I tried to read a book about the Kent coast I bought years ago but never got around to reading. I couldn't concentrate. The train crossed the border into Wales, another country, sun streaming through the windows.

Coast, City, Country

In these woods I can see the future. Helena rubs her belly-bump. She seems excited. She was always precise with her words, careful not to waste them in idle chatter, and I like her that way. I always did. She'll speak her mind when she knows it, not before. Nothing changed as everything changed. She says she doesn't enjoy visiting her friends in East London anymore, the routine once-a-week ceremony she has with her best friend Sofia withering. We left the city and many of our friends for almost three years, went to live on the Kent coast in cheap expansive housing in a dilapidated resort town, a life of salt and watery amnesia, exactly what we needed at the time. We learned, there, how to slow down and adapt to the rhythms of a sea so different from the city. Long ago, as a couple we agreed we were people of the city, the coast or the country – never the suburbs. Friends would periodically come down to stay, marvel at the cheaper beer, the sand grains stuck between their toes, and sometimes they bought driftwood sculptures by local artists to put on display in flats back in the capital. We travelled occasionally to the city for birthdays, a New Year's celebration, the christening of my sister's firstborn.

We moved back three months ago, and then, to the dismay of all our friends, to Kilburn not Hackney. Here we were, today, escaping out to Wales for a week, already an itch to escape the city on a regular basis in a way we never had before. I like *returning* to London, that's the only way I can put it. Naive to think our old routines could just be picked up, as if we weren't older. As if her belly didn't swell.

Helena has drifted from her friends. I know this hurts my wife in a way she cannot, or will not, articulate. I have no idea whether she's told Sofia the news. I feel it's not my place to ask. Things, times, people change, I say to her, knowing I'm spouting platitudes and ashamed of my clichés. But what else to say? We only become more like ourselves as we get older.

'Dan!' cries Helena, wandering off ahead while I stare skyward at the wheeling kite. 'Dan, come see this!'

'You don't see them in Kilburn,' I say gesturing at the kite, beaming, and striding toward her. I sound like my dad.

'You get them in Chesham, Si, it's not that special.' She's right; end of the Metropolitan Line out in Buckinghamshire the kites are ten-a-penny, successfully reintroduced; once nearly extinct and shunted to the peripheries of Wales, now as common as the kestrel and buzzard. If it makes seeing them less of an event, so be it.

Llyn Clywedog

Up by Llyn Clywedog reservoir the kites are plentiful, wheeling over the still black water. Yesterday we ate sandwiches and drank milky coffee at The Red Kite Cafe, looking out over that flooded valley where old farmhouses sleep under black water. From the cottage, we walked into the nearest town, Llanidloes, through its tiny market square past a few pubs with locals and tourists already outside drinking and smoking, enjoying early summer. In the local hiking shop we picked up a badly designed leaflet marking out the route of the Sarne Sabrina route, a route that would take us up to the sleeping black reservoir. We found the starting point behind a half-empty car park, where a statue of the Celtic river goddess Sabrina, spirit of the Severn stood a few metres from an overflowing bin. A spider's web connected Sabrina's ear to shoulder. I looked at our crude map. Helena swigged her water. We set off.

We walked through farms, saw handwritten signs warning that dogs off leads would be shot, next to photographs of disembowelled sheep. Helena lay down in one field among daisies and buttercups, the land falling away behind her into rolling hills with no other human in sight.

Bent Branches

The man who rented us our cottage, Darran, is a cheerful ex-Londoner with a dangling CND earring that Helena scoffed at the second he disappeared. He told us a few tales of the area, how a car carrying three generations went off the road into that black water a few years back. A little girl was murdered in a town ten miles away, her death plastered across last year's red-tops. The days when this area was part of the nineties free festival scene, pubs with signs outside saying NO

PUNKS NO HIPPIES, thieves rustling sheep in the night and shipping them over to Ireland, trouble with the gypsies.

I replay his stories as I follow my wife across the dry clearing. Now, for the first time, I'm seeing the world in terms of its negative potentialities. Soon, we'll have something to truly lose. On a day of such beauty and sun, I struggle to not think of death around me, the mortality of trees, spectral hounds, the endless regeneration and rebirth that keeps the world going.

I catch up with my wife. After three years, it still strikes me as odd to put it that way. She wanders a few metres off the path into disordered undergrowth, a sound like scrunching old newspapers as she wades through the leaf litter.

'Look.' Her left hand, wedding ring glinting green light, clutches a bent branch. My eyes refocus: it's like one of those dreadful magic-eye pictures from the nineties, and what she sees I suddenly see. Branches arched, entwined, held firmly in place with string and plastic ties. Bearing no load, only ceremonial. Here, today, in this wood, it feels right. I'm not a religious man but somehow this feels right. It's in context.

'It's a chapel, Dan. A tree-church, or whatever they call it.'

'They?'

'The hippies. The pagans, wiccans, whatever. That's what it's got to be, right? Maybe Darran comes up here with his wife and kids!' She rubs her belly and makes a sardonic peace sign with her left hand, her wedding ring obscured by green shadows.

'I hope so. Else we've stumbled on some Welsh *Blair Witch* action.'

She throws a clod of earth at me. 'Shut up.'

Peace

We met eight years ago. So long and the blink of an eye. Now that it, the *baby*, is growing, I fret about how we'll edit the story of how we met, whether the facts should be blurred, the narrative tweaked. Do I even remember it all correctly? What kind of *other* parents will we meet and will I like them?

I liked her immediately: she hated the word *creative* being used as a noun, smoked American Spirit with liquorice Rizla and leaked blue smoke out the corner of her mouth. She said things I thought wonderful, like *you can't buy authenticity*. She had family in Hobart and Sydney, whom she used to visit as a child. She wanted to go again and, four years later, we did. She bought a crappy fluffy souvenir of a thylacine in a gift shop, garish yellow with cartoon stripes. Hard to remember that the creature was once real, was talked about in the present tense. I think she still has it, buried with our life's ephemera in a cupboard somewhere. Something for the kid to play with. She was into green politics, then, and still is, really.

In the edited story do I tell the child how many beers I'd sunk, what her mother and father snorted off the smeared glass table of a mutual friend, what my mental state was, how we ended up in bed not even knowing each other's surnames? I was 26 and she was 24. There were ups and downs, and eight years rolled by. People think a child might bring a bit of focus, stability, peace. I want peace, I say to myself and to my wife, but the word is so hard to pin down. Peace as contentment, stagnation, boredom? To be at peace, I tell myself, is to be dead. To sleep under black water in a flooded valley.

Stories

Helena sits on a mossy log underneath the bent branches and pulls a quizzical face for the camera as I record our memories; I have this terrible nostalgia for the present. I project a future-image of myself remembering this day, pulling up the files on a tablet, a laughing toddler bouncing on my knee. In the woods, I can see the future. Helena's bump is just visible. The dappled green light makes her face unknowable. I pass her the camera.

Here in Wales it's easy to slink off into sylvan fantasies, fair folk of the Celtic hillsides, those bounding phantom hounds, portals into other dimensions and narratives structured so differently from the ones I was schooled with. I grew up on a diet of Grimm and Hans Christian Andersen, before I graduated as an eager child on to mythologies outside of Northern Europe, the sometimes inexplicable tales of the Celts where I learned of titanic aquatic beasts like the Afanc, the charming trickster coyotes of the Native Americans, malevolent kappa in Japanese rivers and condor rides over the Andes to find a lost star-bride. I have to remember these stories, all these stories that meant so much to me, and pass them on.

I've read *Porius* and *Sheepshagger* and *The Great God Pan*. I find comfort in ideas of old ways persisting, eruptions of pagan rites through dirty cracked concrete. I say I'm a rationalist, an atheist, but these things have an undeniable pull. This church of bent branches is not helping and I pull Helena away, who is still snapping away at the thing with her camera from every conceivable angle.

We explore Pen Yr Allt for the rest of the evening until dusk draws in. We exit the wood onto an empty road, no pavement, that leads us down back to the cottage. Only two cars pass us on the walk back, and one tractor.

The evening passes with a single whisky. I nip out and have a solitary rollie, I'm trying to quit. She's had to quit and so must I. I want to. I stoke the fire, we watch crap on the television, and I feel at peace.

Hafren

On our last day in Wales we visit the pine forest. Darran has kindly offered to drive us around a few of the sites that are beyond walking distance, knowing we don't have a car. I enjoy his company and I think Helena does too despite her mockery. She sees something that she may have been herself, or may become, and she reacts against that.

I sit in the front seat of the car with Darran and we chat about bands we've both seen or liked, stuff from the old squat and free festival scene, he's into stuff like Blyth Power and The Mob, Culture Shock and Radical Dance Faction.

'I wish I'd been around for those festivals. I was too young.'

'It got a bit much after a while,' he says. 'Once we had this hippy chick staying on our sofa for five weeks, never paid any rent or cleaned up, and when she wasn't away with the fairies she was on speed.'

A thought strikes me. 'Do you know the guy who walks those massive dogs up in the woods above the cottage?'

'No, never seen him,' replies Darran.

In the back sits Helena with Darran's eight-year-old son, Iestyn, talking incessantly at my wife about everything from the ice-giant in his *Beast Quest* books to the murdered girl in the next town along and he asks Helena if she can sing the Welsh national anthem, at which point all three of us adults burst out laughing as Helena, flummoxed, apologises that she can't. Iestyn simply shakes his head, genuinely disappointed.

We drive once more past the Llyn Clywedog reservoir, the water black obsidian. I squint and see a few backpackers resting outside The Red Kite Cafe, rucksacks at their feet. They stretch sore limbs, looking up at the soaring kites. The water holds its secrets. No water spirits live there.

We pull into a deserted car park, the entrance to a vast and silent pine and spruce forest. Hafren. I step out the car and dutifully read the information sign. The forest was planted in 1937. My grandmother is older than this forest, predating Hafren by twenty-one years. Somewhere near here is the source of Afon Severn where Sabrina must now sleep, under the peat bog where the river rises. Shrouded in this forest are Bronze Age copper mines, and somewhere we can walk to the place where 'The Severn Breaks Its Neck'. I want to do all of this, see and understand all of this, and we have no time. Iestyn runs into the trees, his dad cheerfully reminding him not to go out of sight. Helena walks chatting with Darran. I lag behind clutching the camera, looking for a perfect shot. It looks like a forest. How can an image capture the emptiness? Hafren has no birdsong, no undergrowth to speak of bar moss and sphagnum, the soil acidic and hostile to unprofitable plant life. In this terrifying imitation of woodland, no branches are bent, no ceremonies undertaken, no stories told. No memories can be formed. I can't see the future.

I step off the raised wooden path to look closer at one of the trees. I blink. The forest shifts and warps. I look around, trying to find Darran, Iestyn, Helena. Nothing.

Only silence.

Gary Budden

X.
An Exhibition

The City

Sirens and shrieks in the gloom. Somewhere out there, glass shattered. I listened to the night as I packed my bag, a few changes of clothes, toothpaste and soap, a tongue-in-cheek book on punk rock and genre theory. I phoned my father and told him when I would arrive the following morning. He agreed to pick me up from the station; we would drive the rest of the way.

I slept fitfully and alone, beset by muggy dreams of ancient coastlines, Victorian bathers in pornographic poses, an immediate family who never visited.

Morning came with weak summer light. I got ready fast, grabbed my bag and headed to the tube station. Commuters were already doing their daily grind. Their faces were inscrutable, locked down, as was mine when I was en route to work. I listened to loud hardcore to block out the city.

I arrived at the station, sweating slightly. I bought an overpriced and greasy pasty and bit in too early. The filling burnt my tongue. Notice boards reconfigured with the correct information and I boarded the train, to take me out of the city, to The Exhibition.

The Train

The train was largely empty. I read my book, munched my pasty and drained my coffee.

The city ebbed away and my home county began, the land flattening out as green overtook concrete and the suburban conurbations faded into farmland. I gazed at grazing cows. I read about a black fox sighting in a discarded *Daily Mail* I found on the seat adjacent. A sign of ill-omen in British folklore, it said. A photo of its dead and battered body, snuffed out by traffic, stood as the article's centrepiece.

An hour and twenty minutes passed, and I reached Herne Bay station. I stepped out to greet my father on the platform, we hugged, said how good it was to see each other. I was surprised to discover that I meant what I said.

The Drive

This was a rare trip out of the city back to the homelands. My father was pleased I was there. I hadn't seen him in six months.

We shared many similar interests and would chat every few weeks over the phone about how the Tories were gutting the country, of how West Ham were doing, what interesting documentaries we'd been watching on BBC4. I'd nod and smile as he repeated that things now were the same as – no, *worse* –

than the early nineteen eighties when I was born. He had said this many times before, as if repetition made his point stronger. But what he said was true, I had to concede that. When we met in the flesh, conversation became more difficult, divergent cross purposes and overlapping sentences, endless tautologies and no substance. I hoped The Exhibition would burst the dam. On the phone, describing The Exhibition, he was more enthusiastic that I had heard him in years.

It was a short drive to Margate, my father talking of local events and family members who I never saw and thought about even less. BBC Kent mumbled softly on the stereo about local traffic issues, the effect of the Crossrail, an upcoming Oyster Festival on a more fashionable stretch of the coast, and The Exhibition. Local pundits discussed how this would benefit the area. The word 'bohemian' was used. The coast was hidden for most of the short drive, as I daydreamed of Kentish selkies, mermaids and sirens.

We passed a giant structure named Thanet Earth, the UK's largest, most high-tech greenhouse complex, according to my father.

Drizzle speckled the windows as we drove up the Thanet Way, past St Nicholas-at-Wade roundabout and onto the Canterbury Road through Birchington. The houses we passed were dripping in Union Jacks, bunting hanging like rotten fruit off the houses. Cheap plastic nationalism beaded with condensation. The royals had been up to something of late that seemed to make people happy, of that I was sure, but I struggled to remember the details. This coast made me an amnesiac and fretful.

'Lot of Union Jacks,' said my father.

The next town on our route, Westgate, was much the same. Here, more St George's crosses flapped in the breeze than Jacks. Everywhere, the bunting.

Finally, we reached the town, the sweep of the coastline stretching away in front of us in a majestic curve, the harbour visible with a few boats bobbing on the waves. The Gallery, our destination, stood solitary and metallic in the distance. To our right, a towering block of flats stood guard over a half-built Dreamland. A temporary black-and-yellow sign stuck to a lamppost pointed the curious in the direction of the 'Margate Museum of Monstrosities'.

We parked up in sight of the beach, paid the modest fare, and headed into The Old Town. That was the quickest route, my father said, unless you wanted to cut through Primark. I wrinkled my nose at the thought.

The Old Town

We entered The Old Town.

A public information point, rendered in tasteful black and gold and carrying Margate's coat-of-arms, proudly announced:

1736 – ENGLAND'S EARLIEST SEASIDE RESORT – 1736

I dutifully took a photograph on my iPhone for my records. I scribbled the info in my notebook. My father had already passed the sign and was striding ahead.

Red and yellow-beaked herring gulls were flitting anxiously in the rooftops. They screeched incessantly and pirouetted above the sluggish rooftops, their shit covering the peeling messages that informed of *Thanet's Best Sport* and *The Weekend's Best News*. I stared up at the sky as my father surged ahead, enthusiastic in the faint drizzle. This grey and pervasive damp was reassuring English seaside weather. I wrapped it around myself, comforted by the drizzly panacea. I couldn't recall this place ever being sunny, or warm. The town, like the host-country, didn't exist without the patient rain.

One of the gulls launched off a terracotta chimney with an ear-splitting cry, heading in the direction of the murky sea. We, however, were heading in the direction of The Exhibition. An old woman, her outfit a rainbow of pastel shades, shuffled by, her gaze directed with bored curiosity toward me. As I looked away, ashamed, I noticed a bunch of discarded yellow carnations, lying in a dustbin.

'Come on,' shouted my father, not unkindly, now a hundred feet away.

My foot snagged on some greasy chip wrappers left as appeasement to the gulls. I shook it off, and followed my father. I could feel the old woman's gaze on me.

Running after him, I noticed a glut of small boutique stores, selling hand-crafted jewelry, local art, handwoven objects of no practical use. The shops looked empty.

I thought about Helena.

The Dreamtime

Helena was a friend with artistic tendencies made in my mid-twenties in The City. Margate was the place of her birth. In a city where everyone I met was Polish, Finnish, Canadian or Colombian, this was unbearably exotic. In the years before we had met, I would lie in the siren-shredded multicoloured night, trapped in squalid bedsits, thinking erotic thoughts about mythical women from the home counties, scantily-clad beauties from the Garden of England, with thick estuary accents in states of incandescent arousal.

Helena had tattoos, cobalt-blue hair, the standard black clothing and patches. A malachite necklace always hung low around her neck. She was a fan of hardcore punk, epic crust and post-metal. I suggested to her that it was a male-dominated subculture – what did she see in it?

'Sometimes,' she answered, 'I *hate* my interests.'

We would talk of that seaside town, neither of us sure if it still existed, of Dreamland and Albion's dreamtime, our myths of an arboreal past, gritty sand, sad childhood memories of Kent and the early nineteen-nineties, antediluvian visions of the town before the floods of 1949. We shared history here. She'd tell me about her favourite sea monsters, talk about Margate, USA, near Atlantic City and I would nod without fully understanding, but would sing a bit of Chas and Dave:

'You can keep the Costa Brava and all that palava, going no farther, me I'd rather have me a day down Margate with all me family.'

One summer we had travelled through the old Cinque Ports, climbed down their Limbs kicking our feet through salt spray, sand and shingle. We stood firm and picnicked on the silted land that was once the Wantsum Channel. We searched in vain for memento moris of an absent sea. We clambered over Roman ruins, National Heritage audio-tours blocking out the cries of the gulls, ate sandwiches in Sandwich with Pfizer chemical plant austere in the background. We stayed at my mother's, on the coast, where we drank tea, ate more sandwiches and exchanged pleasantries. Since The Exhibition, much has changed.

In the city, Helena and I sat on curb-sides outside of punk shows with the rest of the voluntary outcast, swigging Special Brew from stolen cans.

'Did you know Buster Bloodvessel ran Fatty Towers in Margate? It closed back in '98,' I always asked when half-cut.

'I know,' Helena said, 'you've told me that before. A place for fat cunts.'

I was a broken Trojan ska seven-inch.

The Skinheads

Margate had its very own skinhead shop. The question of how it turned a profit fascinated me, but the rents, I noticed, as I wandered through The Old Town with my father, were very low. Many shop fronts were boarded up, nestling next to blooming gastropubs with embarrassed architecture.

We entered the shop, Desmond Dekker's *Israelites* leaking out of the stereo as a huge bald man in a 2-Tone T-shirt nodded silently along in assent. I was not a skinhead, but the Harringtons appealed. I had read Richard Allen with some interest, owned Doc Martens, and listened to The Oppressed and other anti-fascist Oi! The *Trojan Skinhead Reggae Collection* was a saved playlist on my Spotify.

Posters of The Specials, The Beat and Madness, adorned the walls. A vinyl reissue of The Last Resort's *Skinhead Anthems: A Way of Life* sat on the counter in stark red, white and blue.

The adjoining shop catered for cybergoths and the psytrance crowd. I didn't really know what it was. Dance music and I had a fractious relationship, but when pushed I would dance with chemical enthusiasm to dubstep and drum'n'bass. The girl at the desk was an attractive day-glo rainbow with hanging dreadlocks and a faint smile. Did she actually *live* here? I was too timid to ask.

I thought of Helena, long disappeared now. Where did she go? Surrey, East Lothian or the Gower, perhaps. She was born here, but I was birthed onto the tarmac of the North Circular, then shuttled down a few years later to develop in a land of saltmarshes, rusting arcades, bowling greens and, as the years went on, day trippers from the city. I fought it, but this was the place I still thought of as home.

Helena could always sidestep this problem. She was fine with loving the city and the coast equally. Both things informed her and her work. She claimed there was no tension or contradiction within her. The city and coast were simply different areas on her psychic map.

'If the city were by the sea,' she stated, 'then that would be perfection.'

I rolled my eyes at this, but in the years after she left, I slowly gained some understanding. All the places I visited became one place. Scafell Pike, Lindisfarne, Stodmarsh, The Hole of Horcum, backstreets in Manchester, Birmingham's Bullring, the city walls in York, Pegwell Bay, the Thames Barrier, these were all significant parts of my life, hard to pull apart and rank in order of importance.

But by the time I realised this, Helena had been out of my life for years. I no longer even had an email contact and Facebook searches yielded nothing. It was a rare skill to truly disappear.

The Seafront

My father and I exited the skinhead store, leaving The Old Town, passing a shabby and thronged Primark, ice cream vendors in catatonic states, and fungal restaurants. We found ourselves confronted suddenly with the grey sea, too cold today for swimmers. The long arcade was our route to The Exhibition.

It stretched for miles, Victorian lamp posts lurching out of the pavement, young couples arm in arm laughing with each other, a muttering homeless man swigging cider on a promenade bench. The glittering arcades flashed neon and promised more than they could give.

'What is The Exhibition, really, Dad?' I asked.

'You'll see. You'll love it, Son.' I clutched the vinyl copy of *Skinhead Anthems* I had purchased.

On we marched towards The Gallery.

There were ongoing debates whether The Gallery's energies were regenerative or vampiric. I had my plan, my plan to hate it and assume the standard anti-posture. It was expected of me. I had to visit the place to do this convincingly, and yes, I was aware of my hypocrisy, my lack of purity, my inability to *ignore*. I fed The Exhibition and The Gallery with my own pointless discourse and they grew plump and healthy on scorn and disapproval.

Bored herring gulls hung in a sky suspended as we entered the cavernous gate that led into The Exhibition. Strangely uniformed attendants stood watch, fiddling with their mobile phones and not quite looking at us.

'We're here,' stated my father, bursting with pride and satisfaction that he'd lured me down from the toxic city of his youth, of my adulthood.

Rodin's *The Kiss* welcomed us into the building. To its right, curiously, was the gift shop, situated before The Exhibition.

Groups of tourists milled around, examining tote bags, flicking through heavy Taschen hardbacks, and browsing the selection of postcards on a squeaky spinner. I heard Philadelphia accents, murmurings in Japanese and German. Many, many voices like my own. Women uttering their erotic estuary vowels. My mind was flooded with images of tattooed women in Victorian bathing suits, frolicking in brine while the Industrial Revolution played out in the background, all set to a skinhead ska soundtrack. To control myself, I focused on a badly designed guide to the work of J.M.W. Turner.

My composure regained, we entered The Exhibition.

The Exhibition

I stepped inside. Immediately to my right was a grainy photo portrait of a young Arthur Rimbaud.

The ceiling was miles above, half-tame herring gulls wheeling and screeching, enjoying the warmth. They were modernising, moving with the times in a way that I never could.

Gull shit occasionally splattered on the floor, on the exhibits, and on us. A fat blob of guano landed on my Last Resort LP.

'Bollocks!' I hissed. My father shot me a look.

'Look,' he said.

Spread out in front of us was a psychic map of Britain. A map of everything I ever held dear.

A kraken tentacle, allegedly washed up on Margate's shore in the mid-nineteenth century, floated in a tank of preservative fluid a hundred metres high.

A wall, every able bit of space used, displayed an exhaustive record of British counter-culture in the seventies, eighties and nineties. I was staggered.

'I told you you'd like it,' laughed my father. I was thrilled that he still knew me so well.

The weight of information, the visual barrage, nearly buckled me at the knees. Kentish accents murmured threateningly in the distance. An American woman, shrill with culture, ignored the signs and snapped away on her iPhone camera. None of the attendants bothered to stop her. Slogans from my past, our past, were everywhere.

CLASS WAR. CHARIOTS OF FIRE!

Charles and Diana peering out of a gaudy Union Jack/ Butcher's Apron.

A poster of Duran Duran.

An original poster advertising anarchist punk band Conflict. WAR ON THE STREETS, it declared.

WHO DO THEY THINK THEY'RE FOOLING? YOU?

Angelic Upstarts, The Clash, FREE THE H-BLOCK PRISONERS, Cockney Rejects, grotesque Thatcher caricatures, a promo poster for The Raincoats.

Prickles licked up my spine as I saw an old Skrewdriver badge. Nasty Nazi pamphlets from back in the day, *Blood and Honour,* Combat 18 totenkopfs, skinhead bootboy violence, boneheads, the rotten side of all this.

Whoever had curated The Exhibition had gathered this underground ephemera, really knew their stuff. I was envious and impressed.

My father, smiling, led me to another part of The Exhibition. There were pictures of me, my younger brother and sister at various stages in our development. Holding Christmas presents. Smiling in school orchestrated photographs. Standing muddy in a campsite in the Lake District somewhere near the base of Scafell Pike. Birds of prey grasping leather bound arms at a falconry outside of Oxford.

I wish I knew where my brother was, what my sister did with her time. In that moment, their absence was palpable. Kent dwellers as they were, they saw my mother and father regularly. I had not seen them since Christmas two years ago.

My mother featured in none of these photos, and I struggled to picture her face in my mind's eye. I thought of Helena and I, sipping tea with her in Whitstable on a rainy summer's day before a cycle trip to Reculver.

Another wall: a painting of Victorian bathers, accounts from old punks and skinheads, portraits of them now in middle-to–pushing-old-age juxtaposed with them caught in the frames of blurry Polaroids as teenagers, young men and women. Typed up accounts of what it all meant to them clung like lichen to the walls; trips down to Margate to indulge marginal cultures in a marginal place. Didn't they realise that they'd been imprisoned, compartmentalised, made a part of a history they never wanted!

But what did I know. I was a middle-class pretender and a parasite. Maybe they realised, and didn't care, or relished this delayed appreciation. Helena once told me our memories stretched back as far as our ancestors. I hadn't seen her for years but thought of her every day; we were never even lovers.

I always made a point of going into exhibitions, plays and movies, blind. I said it made it fresh. I wondered why an artful photo of Helena, drunk, was a part of the display.

I was soon answered. The next section of The Exhibition was devoted entirely to the work of my once-and-future friend, Helena Williams. I read a gushing biographical blurb neatly typeset onto the wall of The Exhibition in a modern, progressive font. The errant prodigal daughter, returned to the 180-degree town of her youth, was the mastermind of The Exhibition: curator, exhibitor, artist, saviour. Everything she was needed to be.

I paused to stop and examine a set of line drawings titled *Anthropological Study of the Kentish Male, Removed From His Natural Habitat, The City, 2005.*

There I was, rendered in charcoal, can of lager clutched in fist, outside a sketch of a pub in New Cross. She'd made me look thinner than I was in our real life, and I was grateful for that.

My father joined me.

'That's you, Son,' he said.

'I know, Dad, she was my friend.'

'Who?'

I sighed.

Elsewhere I was treated to *Salt Woman*, a bizarre self-portrait rendered in dyed salt crystals. *Anthropological Study of Kentish Female, Margate Seafront, 1998*, depicted a young woman drunk and alone on a wintry coast. *The Last Resort*, was a collage with unsettling fascist skinhead imagery. *The Kraken of Kent, Ice Cream Ossuary, Memories of Meregate, Giving up the Coast, Cinque or Swim, Re-degeneration* and *The Dreamtime/Ben Bom Brothers.* A disturbing and inspirational collection. The work of, I realised, a major talent. I was proud.

She'd been prolific in the time since we'd last seen each other. I had done nothing but drink and lose myself in psychedelics looking for an Albion I knew wasn't there.

We spent a good hour in Helena's room. I hoped there were prints available. *Anthropological Study of the Kentish Male, Removed From His Natural Habitat, The City, 2005* would make a good postcard. I could send one to my mother.

In the gift shop, taken with The Exhibition as I was, I rushed to buy the accompanying book. It was plump with observation and discourse, and printed on heavy paper. Reproductions of Helena's work stood in full colour in the centrepiece. The girl behind the till uttered the phrase 'ten pounds' with such sultry southern English vowels that I became a babbling mess. My father just shook his head. I handed over a crumpled note and hurried away.

We left The Exhibition, left The Gallery, and headed to the nearest pub, with a view over the grey sea where we ordered ourselves pints of lager and portions of greasy cod and onion rings. My father started talking about a recent birdwatching trip. I gulped down alcohol.

The Last Resort

That night we ate bombay aloo, tarka daal and chapattis and drank cold canned lager. I slept on the sofa. In the morning, I boarded a train that sped me back into the city.

On the train, desperately trying to ignore a group of late-teenage girls who sat drinking and planning their daytrip in the metropolis, I recalled the last time I'd seen Helena.

I knew she was leaving. I pretended not to care. We necked Jägermeister, dabbed powders out of a dirty plastic wrap, and watched a local punk band who we agreed were shite. One last chance to experience nothing changing.

We talked about parents, how we defined ourselves and the places where we grew up, of how she wanted to pursue her art and realise some of the crazy thoughts she had running through her head. I had always encouraged her. I said to her that I thought the whole punk subculture may have some life in it yet, room for more stories. Who got to put the final full-stop on the narrative? She nodded enthusiastically. She talked of how she wanted to leave the city, do something different, that she was never going to focus on her art in this place. She needed salt and shingle.

'Remember the Wantsum Channel?'

I nodded sadly.

'I want to go home,' she said.

'I understand,' I said.

She was the last woman I ever knew with that accent.

We said goodbye as I put her on a crowded night bus. I waved as the bus pulled away and into the heaving traffic. I bought a can of cider from the local off-licence, and walked home through the city.

XI.
Coming on Strong

I'm at the bottom of a grassy bowl a few miles out from Winchester, the blazing sun dipping crimson below farmland that stretches out for miles beyond the fenced perimeter. Jacketed young men and women lean bored and fluorescent against metal mesh fencing. Half of them, at least, are volunteers, supposed to be stewarding the crowd. They're only here for the free ticket the two shifts they've signed up for guarantees, high-vis revelers on pause, doing a bad job and unsteady on their feet. Everywhere I can smell the mingle of warm earth and green grass squashed underfoot, the sharp sweat of a thousand unwashed, blue cigarette smoke, spilled cider, cut with countryside breeze and flecked with pollen. Trees have a smell and I can smell them.

PK's laid on the yellowing ground, arms stretched like a dropout messiah, trying to leave a lasting imprint on the earth. He's grinning to himself, exhaling smoke and staring up into the sky. Dub from a nearby tent sends shockwaves through the soil.

I can feel it in my bones. Living things dance in the air. I crush a mosquito that feeds on my intoxicated blood, its body smearing across my skin.

'PK, get up you wally!' I shout, not really meaning it. I'm just happy to be here, away from Bristol, from the hiss and caffeine of work, from rain and concrete. PK's a space cadet, but he says he loves me. He waves but doesn't get up.

I've got a bit of a buzz on. I want to talk talk talk. About anything and everything.

There's a couple somewhere in their mid-thirties sitting next to me, keeping an eye on their little girl who runs about doing cartwheels and diving head-first onto the yellowed grass.

'She's having a great time!' I say, out of nowhere and embarrassed at myself.

The mother looks up at me, sunlight glinting off her lip ring. She smiles and sort of squints. The dad doesn't seem to notice, his head nodding to a repetitive bass line. Should I think them bad parents for bringing a kid to one of these places?

'First time we've brought her to one of these, she's just about old enough now. It's all a bit of a trip down memory lane for me and Simon, isn't it Si?'

She punches her partner gently on the shoulder.

He looks around, says, 'What, Ade?'

'I was saying to this lovely young thing here, this is all a bit of a trip down memory lane for us isn't it?' Turning to me, 'What's your name darling?'

'Jess.'

'I'm Adrianna. Ade for short.'

She speaks with the flattened vowels and watered-down Cockney of the Thames Estuary. I like her immediately. I sit down next to them and take the cigarette Simon offers to me. Their little girl continues cartwheeling and yelling at the yellow sun.

I explain to them that this is my first time here, how much I'm enjoying it, how I love the music (Oh God, the music! My heart floats), this punk-reggae-dub-ska-folk-rave-jungle-drum and bass. How I've been studying in Bristol and fell in with that city's crew at the anti-fascist gigs in Stokes Croft, parties in the crumbly mildewed squats, veggie burgers in the cafes, dancing the night away in converted warehouses and old factories. A flood of ideas. New causes. Imperialist wrongs and animal rights. How I feel I've uncovered this great secret and want to tell the world about it, how it's making me feel like a better person with a reason to be. I feel like I've found something that's really *real*. Who knew life could feel like this.

'Me and Si, when we were a bit younger than you, we had a great time up in London, those mad parties at The Balustrade before it got torn down and turned into flats. Back in the late nineties this was. We were a bit too young to have done all the free festival stuff, Castlemorton in '92 and all that. God, I wish I could've been there! We went to Bristol a couple of times, too. A party somewhere near Bath, too, if my memory serves, which it probably doesn't.'

1992 is most definitely the past to me, part of a history I'm unearthing. I still can't get my head around the fact it's harder to find out certain things about events in my own lifetime than those from generations ago. 1992 is the year I was born. I tell Ade this and she and Simon laugh.

'Fuck me, we're old!' he says. 'We were, what, fourteen then? I remember when I used to believe in things. It was fun.'

He gets up, stretches, and walks off in search of the toilet.

'Shut up Simon, you miserable bastard!' shouts Ade.

Looking at me, she winks.

'Ignore him. We used to do all that kinda stuff, what you're talking about. Became a bit much after a while though, you know? I left all that for a long time. Had a kid. Found Simon back when I moved back to Kent. Now Jenny's old enough, we wanted to start listening to some good tunes again, you know?!'

'So Simon's not the…'

'No, he's not. Her dad and me separated a long time ago. I know Simon from when we were kids. Funny where life takes you.'

*

PK's roused himself and we're full of energy, walking long rounds of the festival as darkness descends and the real chaos begins. Machine-gun beats, heavy thump of reggae, klezma, Irish folk, all seeping out of the different tents and stages, mixing into a cocktail of vibrating noise. Performers from a fucked-up circus are out in force, stilt-walking harlequins stepping confidently through the crowds with painted grins, fire-juggling heathens, shapeshifters. A mechanical dragon, its neck a straining mass of gears and pistons as it eyes its audience, belches flame into the inky night. We walk through this riot. Tonight, I'm a synaesthete, the music tasting apple-crisp and strong, fluorescent lighting pricking my nostrils with pungent and earthy aromas, the taste of cider a burst of distorted guitar. Ahead, two chainmail figures stand on opposite platforms, blue and red electrical current coursing off them. They swivel, face each other, enact a staged battle of energy and light that I think must be impossible, but there it is, it's real. PK mentions someone called Rayden and a video game. I think of immortals in the heavens flinging lightning bolts on capricious whims and for the first time in my life I feel I've found that other world I was always looking for.

*

Back in Bristol and back to work. It took me a few days to shake the hangover fuzz and the disappointment of being back. But this is my home, I love it here really, it's got everything I need. Family are close by, Mum and Dad still together. PK laughs at me and says I'm the odd one out with a stable family and parents who still say they *love* each other. I feel strangely embarrassed announcing this fact to my new circle. A lot of them, especially the boys, wear their shitty childhoods and the pains they've suffered as a kind of badge. I know a lot of it is bravado, like the lads with shaved heads who talk about football firms with a glint in their eye – like they've ever been anywhere near football violence. They want life to be rougher and more violent – more exciting – than it is. That was the past. At least they've found somewhere they can belong for a few years. I have, and I wasn't even running away. Mary, my sister, only one year older than me, doesn't get this stuff at all. She's into Blue WKDs and TOWIE and clubbing, but she looks so much like me and we have the same sense of humour and I wonder how that can be.

I've friended Adrianna on Facebook. She lives somewhere called Faversham, in Kent. I can visit any time I want, she said. Probably just one of those things people say when they're at festivals, happy and disconnected. I click through a few of her photos from a place called the Hollow Shore, mottled shingle beaches and circling herring gulls, Jenny with bucket and spade somewhere sandy, Simon stubbled and gruff, planting his lips on Ade's cheek. Looking at them I feel a pull towards something. Children? A life-partner? The nineties? All and none of that.

*

The bang-bang of the baristas getting rid of used coffee grounds and the hiss of steam wakes me up. Back at work, asking mothers, businessmen, students, tourists, if they want a pastry with their coffee and do they have a loyalty card? It's enough to kill any remaining buzz I had from the weekend. The pay here's bad, the manager's an arsehole, but it's okay I guess, for now. You're lucky you've got a job, my mother reminds me constantly. Dad stays silent mostly when this subject comes up and I fear I'm disappointing him or that he thinks me lazy. Most of my colleagues are Mediterraneans who speak various levels of English. I've become friendly with a Catalan girl, Sierra. She's from somewhere near Barcelona, originally. I asked her why she moved to England and all she said was that things are worse in Spain. Not the weather, though, I said, and that made her laugh. As soon as I saw the T-shirt she changed into after a tiring shift, I knew we'd hit it off. All stark black and white, FIGHT WAR NOT WARS. It's like being in the masons or something; a secret code that others can spot a mile off. Hiding in plain sight. I don't want to be elitist, I hate cliques, but this just feels good.

'Would you like any muffins or pastries with that, miss?' I ask a middle-aged woman trailing a truculent adolescent and a silent husband behind. The woman looks tired and says, 'No thank you, dear.' I don't bother to ask her about the loyalty card. Will that be Ade and Simon in a few years? Me and PK? A group of students come in with those sanded-down accents from somewhere in the home counties. I'd describe one of the men as a *brayer*. Wearily, I take their order.

*

Friday night. Sierra and I have just finished a long shift, it's already seven o'clock so we dash back to mine and I give Mum a peck on the cheek before we head up to my room to get ready. I stick the stereo on as we take turns to shower, some fast and energetic Spanish ska punk Sierra dug up on Spotify. Mary knocks on the door and jokingly tells me to shut the fuck up and I tell her to piss off and Sierra looks briefly startled but I tell her it's okay, it's just what we do.

We swig from a plastic bottle, own-brand orange juice and economy vodka sloshed together. We don't have much money and this is how we propel ourselves through the nights.

Then we're out into the warm dusk of a West Country evening, the sky retaining a memory of the day's heat, hair done up, jackets on, badges pinned in place. Heading up to The Croft, passing the THINK LOCAL, BOYCOTT TESCO mural, remembering those hooded faces and the smashed glass of a few years back, through the busying streets to meet PK and our mates. It's a warm night so everyone's outside before the gig, swigging from cans of cheap cider, a haze of smoke, some dodgy haircuts and tattooed boys and girls preening like peacocks. When I'm here, doing these things, I feel like I've shed some sort of skin, pulled the rubber mask off to expose who I really am. I can feel that I'm getting closer to something.

*

Adrianna, against my expectations, has stayed in contact. She seems to actually *like* me. She's invited me and a friend, if I like, to stay with them down in Kent. A little weekend visit. It's not a place I've ever been to.

The furthest south east I ever got was a gig in New Cross a year back, staying with one of PK's mates in a disgusting flat near Goldsmiths. I remember waiting at a thronged platform for the Overground, all conversation drowned out by a passing Freightliner with its endless metallic roar, Maersk and P&O rusty containers squealing on the tracks. I had a perverse desire to hop on to one of them, an American dream, just let the train take me where it would.

I jump at Ade's offer. I love being by the sea and I want to explore the country more. Is it odd that I've visited Europe and the USA but not Kent? I mull that one over. I've never seen the Scottish Highlands, the Yorkshire Moors, the Trough of Bowland or the Forest of Dean. I want to. I took PK to Bath; we cycled there from Bristol along the railway path, built over an old track bed. I wanted to tell PK about how I felt about this layering of history, the old Victorian track beds below the soil, on our way to a place with its Roman spas, its Norman sacking, King Offa of Mercia, and us on our bikes. The words didn't come.

I want to ask Ade and Simon questions. They're links in a chain that I want to be part of. She's talked about doing some walks. It all seems so grown up. I choose to go on my own, PK is too much of a liability. I find him embarrassing at times if I'm honest, and Sierra, well, I want this all to myself. Maybe next time.

I catch an early to train to London Paddington, sipping shit coffee from a cardboard cup, battle my way across the underground against unhappy commuters and irritating tourists. This city, it's so big, I travel for an age and still really get nowhere. I disembark at St Pancras, wander around a bit while I wait for the train to Faversham, stand outside looking up at the salmon-pink spires. People everywhere. I smoke a cigarette and say sorry, no, I don't have any change to three different people. Then I hop on the train, a high-speed, and rumble out of London through Stratford (I press my face up against the window trying to look at the Olympic Park, see only harried shoppers and the Westfield logo floating above some sci-fi fortress), Ebbsfleet, which seems to be only a place of concrete, train-tracks and wires, and into Kent proper. Some of it looks nice – green farmland, cows and public footpaths. The train fills with lads with baseball caps and a dog and that sort-of cockney voice. White middle-aged women with short blonde hair chatter among themselves. The overweight ticket inspector has bad breath and I try not to inhale as leans over to inspect my ticket.

*

'So there's this guy, some crazy ex-hippy road-protestor, he hangs out in The Neptune with a pint of Whitstable Bay, wrote this book where he claims that the UK is actually in the shape of a giant angel. Psycho!'

Simon bangs his pint down, the glass imprinted with the Shepherd Neame logo, hoping for laughter. Ale sloshes onto the wooden table. I laugh and Adrianna manages a polite titter. On the table the *Kentish Gazette* absorbs some of the spilt ale, a headline stating APEMAN OF KENT SPOTTED IN TUNBRIDGE WELLS slowly blurring.

We're sitting outside The Old Neptune, a crunch of shell and shingle every time someone shifts their arse, the slow sighs of the rolling sea only thirty metres away. The summer's been good, but today is, even for England, unseasonably hot. Chubby-armed men and women soak rays into lobster-red skin, dogs pirouette in circles of aggression and black-headed gulls float overhead. A child of about five digs his sandcastle bucket into gravelly grey sand and proceeds to tip the contents over his own head.

'Odd kid,' says Simon. 'This pub was featured in *Venus*, with Peter O'Toole,' he announces.

He's already told us this. A pause.

'What do you mean, the UK is a giant angel?' says Adrianna, lighting a cigarette and grimacing.

Dry smoke drifts. Jenny is off near the water's edge throwing pebbles toward the horizon and yelling at something.

'I don't know, I didn't write the fucking book, did I?' says Simon.

'Well, good story,' says Adrianna flatly, rolling her eyes.

Another pause. I look at my feet, swig my ale, fiddle with my piercings. I think of the country as an angel in flight, a trapped giant sleeping beneath the loam and rock. I think of the festival, of the pseudo-Celtic and Anglo-Saxon signs incorporated into the design of LPs I love. I remember a trip we took to North Wales when I was a kid, me and Mary, Mum and Dad. Look at the white quartz, Dad said. That's the remains of the white dragon. The red and white fought, and the red won. I like that story.

Ade watches the gulls.

'Where's Sofia with those pints?' she adds, finally, flinging away her cigarette onto the pebbles.

Sofia is Ade's younger sister. A local artist. Wooden gulls and stuff, driftwood carvings.

Three minutes later, a perspiring Sofia appears with a tray of four fresh pints, beads of condensation sliding down the glass. Whitstable Bay. Ade and Simon live near the Shepherd Neame brewery in Faversham. I'm conscious of my accent down here.

'Alright!' she says.

Her dyed blue hair has come loose and hangs limb-like down the right side of her face. She hands out the pints, looking out to sea as shimmering sun glistens on the burning water. Children splash and scream in the shallows. A serious older woman, cap in place, swims laps further out. Ade's dog, Penny, snaps in confusion at the foam. Jenny throws stones at nothing. On the horizon, a row of concrete towers rise from the waters. The Maunsell forts from World War Two, Simon says, and I nod but don't know what he means.

'They had a picture of Peter O'Toole in there,' says Sofia.

'Simon told us already,' says Adrianna.

*

After I'd arrived at Faversham, Ade picked me up in her battered car. We sat in their house drinking coffee with Jenny looking at me suspiciously and sucking on a lolly, the spaniel Penny (we're both Crass fans, explained Ade) barking his head off in excitement. I looked at what hung on their walls. Gig posters from the late nineties and early two-thousands. A reproduction of a map of Kent, dated 1776. A print from The Gallery in Margate, from a 2012 exhibition by Helena Williams, titled *Salt Woman*. A small framed photograph of Ade in an earlier, more punkish, incarnation.

We decided to take the short drive to Whitstable, swim, wander the fish market, sink pints at The Neptune. ('I'm a veggie,' I said. 'But you must try the oysters,' said Ade.)

The day after, Jenny would be staying at her grandmother's, so Adrianna had suggested we take a trip up the coast, park up near the Herne Bay Downs and walk to Bishopstone Glenn and on to Reculver. Drinks at the King Aethelbert pub. Soak in the scenery, the Roman-ness of it all, the old Church, imagine a lost Wantsum Channel and bouncing bombs, a picnic in the ruins. Sofia said she was hoping to get some good sketches of this stretch of the Kent coastline.

Walking around Whitstable, it seemed that half the population supported themselves from sales of locally themed art. I couldn't picture how she got by. There were so many Londoners here, a lot of French and Spanish, some Americans and Japanese. The streets were packed, tourism was thriving. Were the tourists part of the tourist draw? What is a manmade place in its natural state, I wondered.

*

Sofia grins as she sips her ale. Adrianna frowns. The second round of pints are finally drained and we exit the beer garden in the direction of the fish market on the harbour, pushing through busy crowds. Some sort of community festival is in full swing. The flash and snap of digital cameras surrounds me. On pebbly ground sit a crescent of toddlers, as they watch Mr. Punch insult law and order and upset the status quo.

'My kind of puppet,' says Simon, giving me a wink.

We push on. Next to a teetering stack of sun-bleached oyster shells, another piece of community theatre is taking place. We stop to watch, mingle with the crowd.

A young woman is portraying the part of the Devil. I admire the work of the costume designer, simultaneously evoking images of a cartoonish Christian Lucifer (I think of a crimson tail twirled, arrow-tipped) and older, more threatening pagan beings and the beasts of Hell found in medieval paintings. Sofia whispers to me with a grin that she likes 'that Revelation shit.' I feel grown up in these older people's company, relish the difference of this coastal sunshine to the steam-hiss of work, the sheer drops from Clifton suspension bridge where Dad goes to watch his peregrines. My phone buzzes in my pocket. PK. I don't answer.

An earnest young man with the clean lines and the optimism of a drama student plays the part of narrator.

'Ladies, gents, boys and girls, this is the story of how Whitstable was founded. In the days when Canterbury was a great centre for pilgrimage, its inhabitants grew so rich and sinful that the Devil' – at this he gestures toward the woman in demonic attire, who grins and leers, making one small child clutch his father's leg in fright – 'reckoned he would be justified in carrying the whole town off to Hell. Now, some of you who have ever been on Canterbury high street on a Saturday night probably agree with the Dark Lord on this one!' This achieves the hoped-for result, a small ripple of laughs passing through the crowd. He continues. 'On the other hand, so long as prayers were being said at the shrine of Thomas a Becket, he daren't go near the place. Eventually, after many years, one night the priests at the cathedral were too tired to keep vigil around the shrine. Seeing his chance, the Devil swooped down,' – the devilish actress swoops at the crowd, cries of startled enjoyment erupting from the spectators – 'seized all the houses that he could carry and flung them into the sea off the north coast of Kent.'

Simon looks intrigued and takes a sip of water. Penny sniffs his leg.

We leave the scene of devils and falling architecture, onto the harbour which is cramped with olive vendors, couples clutching mackerel buns smeared with garlic sauce, commercial chatter, idle browsers. We detour through the fish market, polystyrene cups of winkles and mussels, cockles and whelks, dead-eyed sole, skate and bass. The smell of salt and water.

Ahead, I see a group of men and women, coal-blackened faces, colanders on their heads, grasping sticks of sturdy wood. Some grin lasciviously. A gender-bending figure in harlequin attire stands slightly apart from the main troupe, watching the crowd silently before giving a mighty shout that announces the beginning of proceedings. A shower of cockle shells is flung heavenwards as a guitar begins to strum and a woman with pheasant feathers in her hat trills on a piccolo.

'Ade, who are they?' I ask, taken aback.

She laughs. 'The Dead Horse Morris. Bunch of oddballs. Could be worse, they chuck sprouts at you at Christmas time.'

*

Simon, something of an amateur ornithologist it turns out, is talking at length about a kind of bird called a sand martin. He drives the car with Ade affectionately taking the piss, putting on a Kermit-like train-spotter voice saying, 'Yes, yes, they're like the swallows and house martins aren't they, Simon, very interesting.' I know what swallows are, of course, but I choose not to say anything. The stereo plays a compilation of free-festival reggae at low volume. Penny snores on Sofia's lap. I watch this county through the dusty and smeared window.

We drive through a scuffed town in need of a refurbish, Herne Bay, hugging the coast, pass a row of anachronistic arcades with Wetherspoon's drinkers spilling out early in the heat, and up onto the slopes, passing a shit-stained statue of a middle-aged man, where Simon parks the car. I hear the buzz of bees, the rustle of cow parsley. Penny leaps out of the car, barking at two Jack Russells bounding after a chewed tennis ball their owner throws for them.

'Look,' says Ade, and I follow the point of her arm, and see them, Reculver towers standing isolated and proud a few miles up the coast. 'That's where we're going, Jess, we love it up there.'

Up here on the slopes of the Herne Bay Downs I can see far out to sea and Simon gladly points out to me the Isle of Sheppey ('fucking inbreds there'), a glimpse of Essex beyond it, the Maunsell forts once more, the wind farms whose white turbine blades spin slowly.

Five missed calls from PK now. I don't think he'd like it here.

'It's a beautiful bloody day,' says Sofia softly, and she's right, it is.

*

Two hours later we reach the towers, like stone melancholy guardians. I feel in some very real way that I'm at the end of something. This feels like the country falling away, a genuine border between land and sea. For a while I simply sit on the flinty remains of a Roman barracks that have survived these long millennia, dragging on a cigarette and watching Ade and Simon run around in circles with Jenny, making mock monster growls, the little girl squealing with delight. Further off, Sofia sits with Penny by her feet, sketching, looking out over the waves that crash toward the sandstone cliffs, where Simon's cherished sand martins pepper the sky and dart in and out of their tiny tunnels burrowed into the living brown sediment.

I shout to Ade that I'm just off to take a wander, I'll be back in a half hour or so. Want to check out the cliffs. They wave and say OK.

I walk down the path away from the church towers, stop to read a faded information sign picturing an Avro Lancaster, explosives bouncing on water, and a man named Barnes Wallis. Then up onto the clifftops where a path weaves through actual meadowland, small and clearly managed but with skylarks parachuting down into the swaying grasses, insects banging into me, chocolate-brown martins wheeling overhead, and it's bleak here but also beautiful. That feeling I had in a field near Winchester, I have it here also, a feeling coming on so strong that it must be real, the crush of knowledge represented by the barracks and the church, the reggae songs and the tattoos, the martins and the skylarks, Ade and Simon, the bouncing bombs and Clifton suspension bridge, the red dragon and his mechanical twin, the track-bed turned bike path, the shaven headed boys and the lip-pierced girls, Mr. Punch and the coal-faced Morris men, PK and Sierra, Tesco graffiti and shattering glass, Maersk shipping containers and the crush of London, a cherubic being of stone and soil in flight. Here, up on the windswept meadow, in sight of Reculver towers, I get it, and everything connects. The wind whines like the cry of an infant.

Ahead, I see silhouettes of a strange trio standing motionless in front of a small wooden bench. A shawled Roman woman, an oyster fisherman with pots dangling from a shaft slung across shoulders, a World War Two bomber pilot relaxed, at ease, almost cocky. They are two-dimensional, sketched in metal, breeze blowing through their bodies. A house sparrow lands on the Roman woman's head for a moment, I take in its greys and blacks and russets before it flutters off. This trio are mere effigies,

a portrait bench, cast-iron remembrances in a world of amnesia.
I sit on the bench, my back to them, and look out to sea.

XII.
The Hollow Shore

Julie left on Christmas Day. Married for three years, together for five. Upped and left with the gravy and roast potatoes still steaming on our clean new flooring, uneaten evidence of the final argument. What a waste of food.

I drank through Christmas and New Year, taking advantage of the offers on at the local Sainsbury's. I walked by my local library daily, saw its crumbling walls and raw wounds as machines began the demolition. Galliford Try signs apologised for any inconvenience and announced a new cultural centre, luxury apartments, a new cafe. Crane-necked metal beasts ripped out the building's innards and exposed them to dusty air.

Sometimes I stopped and chatted with Tom, the loquacious local drunk who sat on a plastic chair opposite the ruins, offering boozy wisdom to passersby. 'They didn't listen,' is what he said most often.

Eventually a new year came and I returned to work. I filled my free time with books, movies, drink and the occasional line.

I fumbled with a woman ten years my junior in the gents of a gastropub up Clapton, so new the toilet walls were free of graffiti and sexual innuendo. Life as it was rumbled on.

I sat at home listening to the records Julie never liked, at wall-shaking volume, ignoring the bangs on walls from my neighbours. A pile of unopened envelopes grew on the kitchen table. This flat in East London, we'd signed the lease together, split the rent fifty-fifty, the energy bills, the Plusnet, everything. My job paid me a half-decent wage but I was going out more, missing a day of work here and there, using the credit card for everyday essentials. At night, when I finally fell asleep, I waded through waterlogged saltmarsh, mud-spattered and exhausted, running from a black-clad figure that sighed and moaned like the wind behind me. I woke with a splitting headache, hollowed-out, sweating, my tongue sandpaper dry and tasting of ash. I gulped cold water from the bathroom tap, splashed it over my face, stared at a reflection I didn't much care for. On insomniac nights, I sat on the sofa we bought together from John Lewis, now stained with beer and smudged grey, watching films I'd downloaded illegally onto a hard drive. Julie left me most of the stuff, the physical objects we purchased, the *things* we paid dearly for, our accumulated life a list of brand names, furniture, gourmet coffee and organic veg boxes.

I watched English Civil War films, '70s ghost stories, Satanic rituals performed in England's ancient forests. I spent hours at the laptop drowning in pornography. Every morning a new arrears notice stared up from the doormat. Once, I tried to phone her, more out of duty than need. That's what people did in these situations. I heard she was living with a suit who worked in Canary Wharf, weekending at his place in Surrey. She never picked up. I was glad.

By the following winter it was all gone. I was let go when work downsized. I couldn't afford my rent. The credit card bills were piling up. I ignored calls from unknown numbers. Arrears on the water, electricity, gas. Plusnet cut me off. At least I still had the car.

The night before eviction, after a day of piling books and records into the boot, packing clothes and filling out change of address forms, I sat and drank from a good bottle of whisky, stared at my laptop, clicking on sites about the best walking routes in East Kent.

The next morning, I posted the keys through the letterbox, got in the car and drove out through Homerton, under the Hackney Wick flyover through the Blackwall tunnel and onto the outskirts of Faversham.

That's how I ended up living with two ageing people I called my parents for the first time in seventeen years, in an old Victorian house that had been my childhood home, five minutes' walk from Faversham Creek. As I drove, feeling London fall away behind me, my life boxed up in the boot, I felt happy for the first time in months.

*

Early Sunday afternoon, grey. Dad silent in the passenger seat, Mum in the back talking about a friend from work's son's wedding, seemingly to herself. I drove us down the Thanet Way, easing through a patch of floodwater from the recent rains, for Sunday lunch at a venue of their choosing. Harvester. Our first Sunday lunch since I left the city and the first as a trio in many years. I parked up. They went on ahead *to get a good spot* while I locked up. I paused, looking around the sparsely populated car park: bleached crisp packets and fag butts. Felt the rain on my skin and listened to the traffic. A solitary crow watched me curiously, perched in a patch of polluted scrub. This wasn't how I remembered it.

I walked in through the glass doors into the anodyne warmth of the restaurant, an ochre-red antiseptic womb. My mother waved from the good spot they'd secured. I scanned the dining area. Perhaps five other tables occupied. We were here early, *to beat the lunchtime rush*. A young black-haired waitress with a painted smile led me to the table. She took our drinks order and laid down laminated menus as I pulled my seat out. Lager for me, coffee for my parents. The waitress scurried off in the direction of the bar.

'So, how's the job hunt going, Simon?' my father asked, barely looking up from his *Telegraph*.

'Leave the boy alone, he's had a tough year!' said Mum. 'He'll get around to it, won't you Simon?'

Mercifully, the conversation was delayed by the waitress arriving with the drinks. I grabbed mine and took a large gulp. A flash of that painted smile before she disappeared.

'He's thirty-five years old. Not a boy anymore,' grunted Dad as he reached for his coffee. FEARS OVER ROMA MIGRANTS INCREASE, the paper's headline.

I sighed and sipped my pint. 'I'm on it tomorrow. I've only been down a day. There's a recession on, you know. Let's enjoy our lunch together, can we? Come on, have a look and see what you want.'

Mum squinted at the menu, talking away to herself and firing questions at Dad about did he remember what he had last time, and did they still do those lovely fajita-things? I took a quick look, settled on the vegetarian lasagne. My parents took their time. I watched my fellow diners. At one table sat a silent septuagenarian couple poking forks into identical plates of mixed grill. At another, a young mother tried vainly to control the actions of her gurgling toddlers. Her boyfriend, husband perhaps, looked meek and tired and simply smiled as she dealt with the children. In the distance, the bar and service area, where young, white-shirted staff, none more than twenty years old, yawned and tried to look alert for potential customers. Over a weak set of speakers leaked commercial pop music, sugary declarations of love, auto-tuned broken hearts. On the walls hung bleak images of the Kent coast and marshlands: a beckoning black-clad figure distinct in a dwarfing landscape. Crashing waves hitting sandstone by Reculver towers. A portrait of a black curlew, hiding in the reeds. Figures not waving but drowning.

Only one picture I recognised, Dyce's *Pegwell Bay*. I'd seen it in the Tate, with Julie, a few years back. A Victorian family gathered shells, sifted through geological and chronological strata. Donati's comet faintly visible, trailed through the sky. I told my wife about my trips to that same bay as a child, of the fake Viking ship and the hover-port, the shells I collected with Dad. I wondered who made the artistic decisions at Harvester.

'Simon?'

'Yes, Mum?'

'I was saying, are you ready to order?'

'Yep, all decided.'

I swallowed the rest of my pint in three big gulps and beckoned the waitress over. I ordered another lager along with the food, paused, then asked, 'Dad, Mum, why didn't we go to one of the old pubs in Faversham? In Whitstable? There's loads of lovely old places around here with decent pub grub. Good ale. A bit of character. And you choose a Harvester by the Thanet Way?'

My father looked up from his paper. 'We like it here.' For the first time that day, he smiled.

*

I was setting up my stuff in my childhood room. A few Christmases back, Julie and I stayed in here, reveling in the quiet and the pitch-black night.

I ripped gaffer tape off a brown cardboard box that was weighing down the mattress. Old books and LPs, vinyl I'd carried on collecting long after selling all my CDs. I sat on the bed picking through my detritus. *Thunder and Consolation. Avocet. Borderline.* Julie said my taste in music was well out of touch. I liked it like that. I slung books onto the duvet: novels, travel writing, landscape poems, old copies of *Magnesium Burns* fanzine. I flicked through an illustrated guide to British birds, read a random entry on marsh harriers. I found a stash of bent photographs from years back, pictures of me and my mate Dave at a party up at The Balustrade in North London. Dave grinning with his wife-to-be Becky, me with my then-girlfriend Adrianna, her hair dyed, lip pierced, and now a crease splitting her from head to navel. The Balustrade got knocked down years back, replaced with flats and a franchise coffee shop. Memories trapped in cement, waiting to be discovered like sabre-toothed beasts in tar pits.

I carried on unpacking, found an old guidebook I must have bought nearly fifteen years ago. *Esoteric Kent: A Guide to the Hidden Walkways and Roads Less Travelled of the Garden of England.* I opened it up and looked at the publication date. 1998, The Malachite Press. Sixteen years ago. What had changed since then? Was the Thanet Way as busy, had the Harvester already appeared? As I flicked through the book, I came across writing scrawled in blue ink on the title page. *Happy 19th birthday, all the love in the world. Mum & Dad xxx.* I sat on the bed, just holding the book, for a long time.

Only three days here. Housing developments grew in the corner of my eye, concrete putting down underground tendrils like fungus and potentially just as poisonous. More roads, more cars. In the local papers, there was talk of airports in the Thames Estuary, an expansion for the airport at Lydd near Dungeness. I thought of Tom and wondered if he still kept his vigil by the disintegrating library.

Tomorrow morning I was signing on. I decided to do a bit of walking, out from my parents', a long walk through Faversham Creek along the Hollow Shore and onto the pubs of Whitstable. Take a few photographs, get some salty air in my lungs, recalibrate myself. Maybe at the weekend.

That night I sat in my reclaimed room and listened to a few punked-up folk songs on my stereo at low volume. The pictures of The Balustrade had stirred something up. I sent a text to Dave to see if he fancied coming down.

I wondered what Adrianna was doing now. I heard she moved back to Kent. I drank a few bottles of cider, *Esoteric Kent* open beside me, and searched for her online. There she was, so easy to find. Lives in **Faversham, Kent.** From **Faversham, Kent.** I said *fuck it* aloud, and sent the message.

*

Signing on was miserable. Going through my CV, a hollow list of achievements, being told what I already knew, that there were no jobs fitting what I was looking for round here. *I'll be looking for work in London, I'm just staying a while with my parents* didn't seem to register. *Even if you wanted a job stacking shelves in Sainsbury's, which there aren't, you wouldn't get it, because you're overqualified.*

Relieved to be out, I walked into Faversham town centre. It was still early. A few gulls in winter plumage perched on the rooftops. I sat on a bench in front of The Black Curlew pub, looking at the old town hall, smoking a cigarette and eating a vegetable pasty bought from a franchise bakery. I watched people shuffle around the town.

Dave had agreed to come down on Friday. The plan was a couple of pints in The White Fox, then up early the next morning, to walk the Hollow Shore from Faversham to Whitstable. Dave was one of my oldest friends. It was through him I met Julie. They still kept in touch, I heard.

On the other side of the square sat a man in frayed black clothing and heavy workboots, head down and features obscured. He clutched a Tesco bag, smoking a rollup. The word *grizzled* came to mind. He looked like the photographs of men who once worked the shores and creeks of this county, those photographs that stood next to snippets of text on sun-faded and water-damaged information signs, next to spots of historical interest. He barely moved, seemed superimposed, like he'd been badly Photoshopped in.

I watched him awhile before heading back.

*

My parents were out at work. It was nearly midday. I sat on their new sofa they'd recently bought at DFS with the giant flat-screen HD TV playing muted re-runs of *Homes Under the Hammer.* I had the laptop open, with tabs and tabs of recruitment sites jostling for pole-position. Already tired by the job hunt, I picked up my copy of *Esoteric Kent* and looked for the entry on the Hollow Shore: *A particularly good stretch is the marshy coast from Faversham to Whitstable (9.8 miles). It is entirely flat and fairly easy to navigate. Starting at the market square in the pretty medieval town of Faversham, you walk along historic Court Street, which becomes Abbey Street, and then joins the Saxon Shore Way. The walk takes you along creek and shoreline, across fields and past nature reserves, home to a rare breeding colony of black curlew. Eventually Whitstable appears, as does The Old Neptune pub, the perfect place to stop for a pint, before continuing on to tiny Wheeler's Oyster Bar for a seafood feast. Esoteric facts: As part of the Saxon Shoreway, the*

Hollow Shores

Hollow Shore has been the site of numerous ghost sightings over the years with records of an unidentified black-clad figure being spotted out in the reed beds, dating back to the early nineteenth century. A number of sightings from the 1960s also claimed that the semi-mythic white foxes of Kent have been seen along the Hollow Shore, but at time of writing these claims are still unsubstantiated.

I closed the book, clicking my tongue in thought.

On the mantelpiece still stood a photograph of Julie and me on our wedding day, all polished grins and expensive clothing. Julie said I looked like I was due for a day in court when in my suit. I laughed at the memory. I got up and put the photo face down on the mantel. I resumed my job hunt, got distracted, checked my messages. One new message, from Adrianna. In her profile picture, she'd let her hair revert to its natural nut brown. The pierced lip remained. She held a small child in her arms.

Hi Simon, thanks for getting in touch! Can't believe you're back in Kent! You always said you couldn't wait to get away from the place! I heard about you and Julie, so sorry. I'm still in touch with Dave, he told me what happened. Thought about contacting you. Should have. I'm bad at staying in touch.Shall we meet for a coffee? My number is _____Xxx Ade. I replied and arrangements were made.

*

Thursday. Adrianna sat opposite me, steam in the air, coffee machines rumbling and hissing behind the counter. She hadn't brought Jenny, her daughter. 'She's with her dad in Canterbury,' she explained. We were in The Linnet, a tiny cafe, busy this lunchtime. I looked at the woman in front of me and thought of a girl with purple hair and a crease running from head to navel. She looked so different, utterly familiar.

'So how you doing?'

'I've had better years, put it that way. It's good to see you Ade. You know, I found some photos of all of us, up at The Balustrade if you remember it. That's why I got in touch, really.'

'Because of some photos?' She laughed and sipped her coffee. 'Of course I remember it. Long gone now right?'

I nodded, tried to explain.

'No, I mean… I don't know. I saw that you were in Faversham. I guess I realised how long it had been. How did you end up back living here then?' She talked for a long time uninterrupted, winter sun glinting off her lip, explaining how she'd met a guy after me, Danny, how they hit it off in London and spent a good few years drinking and dancing in the grotty venues of New Cross and Hackney ('Before all the coffee shops!'). I knew bits of this story but I didn't interrupt. Jenny was never planned, but at the time Adrianna and Danny were in love and the pieces felt like they were falling into place. Cheaper to move out of the city, they decided. Danny was from Essex, near Canvey Island, but he didn't mind the idea of Kent. They settled in Canterbury. A good place for kids, she said – 'Well we both know that, don't we?' – and I said yes, but possibly a bad one for teenagers. She laughed at that. Jenny was born, things were OK for a bit, then it all broke down, not for any real reason, they were still amicable but it just wasn't working any more.

'Same with me and Julie, really.'

She nodded. 'So, what's it like being back here then?'

'My mother, bless her, drives me up the wall. I need to find work. I should probably be in a worse mood than I am. I'm liking the peace and quiet, planning on do a bit of walking, that kind of thing.'

'You realise how noisy and stressful London is, right? Maybe I'll come with you on one of these walks.'

'That'd be nice. I've got Dave coming down tomorrow, but I'd love to arrange something soon. You can bring Jenny if you like.'

She smiled at that and drained her coffee.

*

Friday. I picked Dave up from Faversham station. I didn't really need to drive and he knew the way to my parents' place – he'd been there innumerable times as a teenager, the two of us smoking weed out the window in my upstairs bedroom, downloading pictures of topless women on the creaky internet we had back in '98. But driving was what adults did.

As I pulled up to the station he was already outside, shivering slightly and looking up and down the street. He probably hadn't been to this town in fifteen years. Behind him, a billboard poster advertised a new installation up at The Gallery in Margate, named merely The Exhibition by artist Helena Williams. Her name sounded familiar. I squinted to read the title of the image they'd picked for this advert. '*Cinque or Swim*', *Helena Williams, 2009*.

I honked the horn. Dave spotted me and climbed into the passenger seat.

'Easy mate, how's things?' We shook hands.

'Not too bad, considering.'

'This place ain't changed much has it?'

'I dunno. Yes and no. There's more people but it feels almost quieter than when I left.'

'No mean feat!' He grinned.

We dumped Dave's stuff back at the house, made a bit of small talk with my parents who asked about Dave's parents, about his son and his ex-wife Becky, how life was up in Lewisham, before we set off on foot out into the Faversham Friday night.

It seemed quiet. Perhaps it had always been like this, when we tried our luck in the pubs as boys. We walked into town back past the station, a group of girls in their late-teens trembling in the cold, pulling inadequate jackets over themselves in a futile attempt to keep warm. Walked onto the market square, The Black Curlew slowly filling with punters. Dodged a middle-aged woman clearly already worse for wear, laying into an exasperated friend, then down a little side alley and through the swimming pool car park onto The White Fox, a decent pub that had been a favourite of ours back in the day.

Dave flung a spent cigarette on the floor as we approached. 'God, I haven't been here in years. Good to be back, actually.'

I nodded.

We entered, the light reassuringly dim. The place still felt like a pub. A place to drink, with a friend. Little from what I could see, bar the free Wifi, had changed in the last fifteen years. Maybe a bit cleaner. The faint smell of disinfectant and piss that all pubs now had, post smoking ban. Like all the pubs round here, it was Shepherd Neame. I ordered two pints of Whitstable Bay while Dave found a seat. The pub was busy but not yet crowded, a few lads either side of the cusp of drinking age furtively sipping cider, a couple of old men in thick jumpers at the bar who stared at nothing in particular, a couple in their thirties with a bottle of red. The barmaid flashed a painted smile as she handed over the pints. On the bar's smooth polished surface were a few cardboard fliers for The Exhibition, sticky with evaporated beer.

Dave had found a decent spot in the corner. It was good to see him. We spent the evening sinking pints, both of us now single, a thought unimaginable when we'd celebrated and laughed *your life's over* at each other's weddings, popping champagne corks, eating expensive canapés and kissing the women who were then our future. He talked about his son and how he missed him, feared for the world he was inheriting, this brandscape that was shutting down any possibility. I talked about my parents and their choice of restaurants, of airport expansions, of Tom and the library, of Julie and our trips to Ikea, John Lewis and Waitrose. We planned our walk along the Hollow Shore from this town to Whitstable, said we shouldn't drink too much we've got an early start, a plan we didn't stick to. The pub filled. Teenage girls sank shots of lurid liquids. Old men mumbled, drank everlasting pints. A fight began between alcohol-pink aftershaved boys, spilling out the door and into the car park with jeers and hoots. Dave laughed, slapped me on the back, cried, 'See, some things round here never change!'

*

We woke early, just before dawn, rubbing nicotine-stained fingers over greying stubble, stumbled to the bathroom for a quick wash, to scrub the sugar and alcohol from our yellowing teeth. I pulled my walking boots on in an early-morning haze. I remembered when I bought them, with Julie, cheap and on offer from our local Sports Direct. *How come there are so many of these places?* she asked once. *They breed like rabbits.* Dave and I clumped down the stairs to find Mum already awake, dressed, brewing a pot of strong coffee and, in that moment, all the times she'd been at that same counter on any cold morning like this, making breakfast for Dad, packing my sister's lunchbox in the '90s, making me some porridge, all came back and I felt guilt and raw nostalgia. I wondered what her life had been like, had it really turned out the way she'd wanted, and why did I give her a hard time about Harvesters and her interminable anecdotes? *I'm sorry, Mum, for everything.* The words ran through my head on a loop, but failed to form themselves on my lips.

Dave gratefully took a large cup of coffee. I did the same, my mug showing an artist's sketch of a black curlew. 'Ta mum!' I said, grinning, wrapping my arm round her shoulder. She was so small. She was happy I was here, I realised.

I packed *Esoteric Kent* into my backpack with something for lunch, a bit of fruit, bottles of water. The walk was only nine miles and we aimed to end up at The Old Neptune in Whitstable by early afternoon for more pints and a decent lunch. We set off, walking into a morning weighed down with mist, through deserted streets onto Faversham Creek, past sleeping restaurants and artisan shops, into the realms of the boat people, a few of whom were already up and active, wraith-like in the mist chopping logs and wrapped in dew soaked fleeces. A woman looked up silently from her chopping as we passed, axe in hand, standing in front of a mildewed boat named *Reynardine*. The mist was a thick, wet swaddling. Boats bobbed on the waters of the creek, the tide low, carved mudflats becoming visible. Turnstones flitted about, gliding in small groups over the creek. I heard the cry of a black curlew somewhere far out on the saltmarsh.

Dave ducked his head as he walked under a large houseboat, *Jack Orion,* propped up on lichened and mossy wooden poles, groaning and creaking like the old men in The White Fox. We came to the end of the boat people's territory, pushed through a squeaking gate and splashed muddy through puddles that dotted the path to the Hollow Shore like some inverted miniature archipelago.

We came to what once must have been a winch for unloading and loading goods, in those hazy days of proud British maritime history. Now, rust patches like orange fungus burst through the flaking white paint, and a hook swung gently on frayed rope. A metallic gallows that stood guard to a rickety wooden bridge crossing the creek. We crossed, looking down the impossible distances to the mudflats where I saw sandpipers dart and dash, and then we were onto the saltmarsh.

We walked and we talked, talked about everything from our childhoods to the abandoned psychiatric hospital rumoured to be rotting out in the Kent countryside, of environmental therapies, the music and books we loved, old memories and fresh stories, the healing effects of horticulture and the debate of town versus city. I told him that I'd met up with Adrianna, and he grinned, but shook his head.

'Do you really want to open old wounds?'

I thought for a moment, and said, 'Yeah, I think I do.'

The path was still sodden from the recent rains, my boots slick with creamy mud, the wind off the Swale increasing its ferocity. This landscape, so flat, barren and beautiful. Icy wind formed tears in my eyes. I paused and leaned against an Environment Agency sign, a litany of danger spelled out in yellow and black; drowning, floods, electrocution, the violence out here easy to imagine.

'Come look at this!' Dave beckoned me over to the concrete wall separating the grassy path from the shore. Bladderwrack carpeted the shoreline before giving way to low-tide mudflats. Over the water, the Isle of Sheppey so close it felt like it was within touching distance. I thought of the prisons there, that solitary bridge connecting the island to the mainland, and the boxing hares I'd watched with Dad when I was nine years old. I saw a black clad figure on the opposite shoreline, waving.

Dave pointed at a small boat that was half submerged in the eager mud, it's prow buried like it was rooting for lugworms. The rust and decay, the ruins and the mildewed boats, these forgotten paths, were too good not to record. He hopped onto the shingle and edged towards it. I watched him clamber and slip on deep-green seaweed as he approached the boat, camera snapping away, spattered mud forming abstract patterns on his jeans. Who would ever have thought the two of us would still be here, in the place where we grew up, post-marriage, muddy as fuck, taking pictures of rusty boats on our smartphones. I was glad we were still mates. Marriage didn't make me happy. Didn't make her happy either. I was happier here than I'd been in ages, dirty, cold and wet. Even the pylons looked beautiful.

I lit a cigarette, watching Dave slip and slide on the bladderwrack. A group of cormorants flapped overhead. I listened to the sigh of the marshes.

The walk continued for aeons, two lone figures, the only ones privy to the giant suspended sky, the shining shingle, the discovery of space in this most crowded of counties. Dave, keen-eyed for ruin, spotted another wreckage, some unidentifiable amalgam of rusted machinery slipping into the marsh, hungry plant life colonising the metal.

'Something they used when people still worked for a living!' he said sourly, before hopping off the path and wading through foot-high reeds to get a better view, smartphone held tight. I heard a wet sucking sound. Dave disappeared. I threw my smouldering cigarette butt into a mud pool, shouted my friend's name again and again. Panic, a thumping heart, cold beads of sweat breaking on my forehead. I tried to calm myself, fumbled for my phone to call someone, anyone. No reception.

An ash-white animal trotted onto the path in front of me, yellow eyes gleaming, its head splitting into a huge canine yawn. It watched me curiously. Further along the path a black-clad figure in heavy, muddy work boots stood clutching a Tesco bag close to his chest, smoke from his cigarette forming a nimbus around his obscured features. He beckoned towards the reeds. I thought of Julie and roast potatoes cooling on brand new flooring , my parents silent in a womb-red Harvester, painted smiles, Tom downing a can of Special Brew as the library crumbled, Dave eyeing up the girls in The White Fox, Adrianna creased from head to navel, black curlews nesting in the reeds, concrete roots pushing deeper and deeper down into the soil, an estuary covered in tarmac, a world of endless flats and cafes.

Hollow Shores

I walked towards him, the white fox following at my heels, hollow and at peace.

Gary Budden

XIII.
Mission Drift

Seven years.

'David, come over here! Food's ready!' Sofia waves at me, grin on her face, wheat-blonde hair hanging low over her shoulders. I've been staring out over the encampment, smoking. I love her voice, that small hint of the middle-class art school weathered by golden sun and cold rain. David loves her. Heat beats down hard on the field. Buttercups radiate gold. Sparrows trill and skitter through trees and bushes. In seven years I've learned so much. I know the names of *things* now, a world so much complicated than *plant*, *bird* and *tree*. Deep down inside, there's a yawning fissure, a crack I can't fix.

David is a dead boy who went under the wheels of a Dover lorry back in '87, age six. David Oldfield, an only son. I am Steven Hunter.

Last time I checked in, some of the lads at the station, the few who knew who David, they asked if I fucked her good and proper, did she have hairy armpits, do the crusty birds smell as bad as the men, what's it like nailing Mother Earth on musty sheets? Lice in her fanny, tofu blowjobs. I smiled, leered a bit, went along with it. Steven laughed, David's stomach curdled. My superiors know about the child.

Today is a day where we *do* something. Shaky with nerves and excitement, even after these seven years. Do the others feel this anxiety, this panic? I sit with Sofia who bounces our daughter Heather on her knee. Heather gurgles and sucks on a rusk. Bolt-cutters lie at my feet and I idly roll a cigarette. My fingers are yellow-orange with nicotine. Before all this, I never smoked. We sit in a rough half-circle with the others, my friends, I suppose. There's Biscuit, a space cadet from Bristol with his theories of astral projection and the redemptive power of super-strength skunk. He expounds on plans for the action. Helena, an eager girl from South London, one of Sofia's close friends, in a baggy and threadbare white shirt, headscarf, DMs. Sofia is from the home counties, Niall's from the Severn Valley and Euan's from County Kilburn. The plurality of the British Isles represented in Earth Now! We profile them and say they are a type. A category. I'm a chameleon. I fit types and tick boxes. I'm drug-dealer, father, husband, activist, lover, law-man. I'm all of these and I'm nothing. I must *look* right. If things had been different… I'm more like them than the society I protect, that distant world that shimmers with unreality.

I fear climate change is real. That's irrelevant, it's not my concern. I have a job to do. My wife, my mum and dad, the kids back home in Brighton, they wouldn't understand. The papers, the TV, they mock them. They mock us. Swampy up a tree. Tie-dye shirts. Laugh, discredit. I see how the police, the public (am I the public?) look at me. I've been told to get a job, cut my fucking hair, take a bath. If only they knew. Would they thank me or would they spit in my face? These questions run laps round my skull at night. In darkness, Sofia sleeping softly, Heather in bed with us, I stare at our nicotine-stained ceiling and think of the little boy, David Oldfield, smeared across tarmac back in '87. I'm David and I'm haunted, a ghoul, a doppelgänger. I fucked her good and proper, they could do with a wash but they ride it 'til it snaps off, laughs Steven in the station. Much more free and open minded, if you catch my drift. There's always laughter at this. Envy, perhaps.

We talk tactics. I often volunteer to lead the action, I've taken a beating and welcomed broken bones from the bobbies to authenticate myself. The looks on their faces as boots hit shinbone, as batons cracked my skull. Real joy. I am them, they are me.

The French have a term, *agent provocateur*. I know enough, have read enough, have been trained enough, to know we've been doing this a long time. Infiltrating anarchists who tried to blow up Greenwich Observatory. They say, in America, it was a provocateur who threw the bomb on Haymarket Square. My old man, he would always tell us that we had French ancestry somewhere. Weavers, protestant refugees who now lie in the Huguenot cemetery in Canterbury.

I rub a hand over my beard. It's in need of a trim, a bit greasy today as I sweat in the June sun. I look at the tattoos that swarm down my arm, a mess of Celtic, Nordic, pagan signs and symbols I chose at random if I'm honest. If I ever go back, I'm scarred with the marks of this life. Yellow fingers and arms fading to blue-green as I age.

They'll break my teeth, smash my wrists if they ever find out. Will I have to leave the country? Perhaps flee to France, over the Channel on a ferry from Dover, pay homage to David Oldfield, make Dad happy and do a bit of family research. They'll not see it that way, but I love this country. I love England and the English, the Welsh, Scots, even the Irish.

When the inevitable happens will I ever see Heather again? She's beautiful but she's David's. The wound I must one day inflict on Sofia weighs me down.

My boots are scuffed and worn. My hair is long. It never occurred to me men could get split-ends. I wear a T-shirt emblazoned with crossed hammer and wrench. I look the part. I hate people like myself. I am them and I'm here to disrupt them, sabotage. I love Sofia, David loves Sofia. I am Steven Hunter.

Seven years. I've touched base camp a few times with a wife and two boys who seem opaque and out of focus, colleagues who I laugh with and disrespect the woman and child I say I love (do love), but it's seven years and that's how long I've been an idea, a character sketch made flesh.

Climate change. I fear it's real. Why would people face arrest, beatings, mockery, sleeping in fields and muddied with earth, if they didn't think it real. Why put yourself at such risk for the sake of an animal. They believe, just as I believe. I have orders, I've got a job to do. There must be dignity in that. What I'm doing is right, for the benefit of my home, the country I love. There are other ways, legal ways, to make your voices heard. We live in a proud democracy, terrorism is not the answer. None of my colleagues are terrorists. I follow my own moral compass and this has to be right.

There are others like me – predecessors, contemporaries – and there will be successors. Rumours of trying to discredit black families in London, relatives of that lad killed by bootboys down Croydon way fifteen years back. The whale lovers. Leaflet-handers outside franchised fast food restaurants. The hunt sabs. I don't know their faces, their names. They must be there.

I cannot be alone.

XIV.
Platforms

The network exposed in daylight is an oddity; where the Jubilee line breaks cover at Finchley Road, I brace myself for a vulgarity of exposed wires and intertwined tracks, the indignity of seeing the true colours of the trains I travel on. Having relocated my life to the north west of the city, I'm still adjusting, wishing the obvious chaos of London was swathed in shadow and easy to ignore, not left out in the sun like an accusation. The colours of my journeys are now grey and deep maroon, sometimes air-conditioned orange, not the bruised black and blue I always felt at home with. I will admit, though, I get an illicit thrill seeing the dirt and coiled cables in natural light rather than the sodium-strip glare of the tunnels. Like a leaked photograph showing a hint of flesh.

Each morning at Willesden Green, the dead platform opposite stares blankly back at me, within spitting distance but always out of reach. Its twin lurks behind. I feel its presence gently nudging my spine.

Elsewhere on the network you have to strain and struggle with a squinted eye to grab a glimpse of the dead stations, the decommissioned platforms, the branches that withered and died. Subterranean zones of the mind's dark night, populated by forgotten cockney troglodytes who worship vengeful gods, the murderous sons of unethical surgeons, transatlantic werewolves and ravers trapped after hours. They're the places that capture the imagination: cinematic, friendly to writers, place-hackers, the swelling multitude obsessed with urban decay.

My useless platforms at Willesden Green are there for all to see, though many don't, not really. They're neither used nor in full disrepair. As such, no one cares.

It took me a while to notice them. With no information signs or wasp-coloured warnings, the dead platforms lack context, remain enigmatic and troubling. Best ignored.

There are shuttered gates, just to the left of the beeping Oyster barriers, blocking access to a redundant stairwell leading down to one of the platforms. Every morning I try and picture it thronged with travellers in outdated clothing, no one fiddling with phones and no tinny noise leaking from their ears. These ghosts wait patiently, some read papers, or novels popular at the time. Some simply stand there, and wait.

The most enjoyable part of my commute is Finchley Road. In the morning, there's a kind of quiet desperation as Jubliee and Metropolitan trains race each other on almost-parallel tracks en route to the station, the only useful interchange for many stops. Commuters come crushing in from Wembley, Watford, as far afield as Chesham and Amersham out in Buckinghamshire. Zone 9? A load of rubbish. I see smart, neat women clutching Kindles, frustrated that I don't know what they're reading. Fat short-breathed businessmen gingerly eye the Met line train, trying to read whether its destination is Aldgate or Baker Street. When the doors hiss open, a mad rush across the platform from one carriage to the other. I've seen fists banged on closing doors and heard shrieks of irritation when the timing is off. Beep beep beep becomes the sound of a morning's failure. Doomed to wait at the platform for another five, six minutes, the foiled travellers pace back and forth like inmates in a yard, sighing as they thumb their phones, eyes darting back and forth from the information board. I never minded myself. If I miss the connection I can soak up the ambience of the station, watch the orange-jacketed staff mumble into microphones, make decisive hand signals, and feel the vigorous ebb and flow of human traffic.

Once, I stood at Finchley Road with a five-minute wait for my connection while a dishevelled man in a creased suit, eyes flaming with cocaine, alcohol and a sleepless night, raved and ranted at us, the commuters. Scolded us for our lack of vision, the paucity of our imagination, how we were all just sheep merrily walking into Mammon's maw. I noticed how his tie hung loose, the knot slack, like in popular American films I'd seen long ago. His skin was greasy and stubble was reclaiming his face. It was 8:45 a.m. and I'd heard the point made before.

I feel a kind of family kinship with my platform. I like to watch the minarets of Central Brent mosque rising above the line of nondescript buildings, aqua-green and off-white, a kind of toothpaste colour. I read cheery signs for Jewish dating websites and ponder what life is like in such unimaginable places as Queensbury and Stanmore. How your whole life could be spent in a place that, to me, is just a dot on a thick grey line. I stand looking at the decommissioned platforms, watching them, waiting for something to happen. They were there, once, to serve the Metropolitan and Bakerloo lines. Now only a few weeds colonise the concrete. Buddleia makes patient inroads. Green parakeets dart overhead.

Two stops down the line, Japanese knotweed got into West Hampstead and they had to level an entire earth bank, razed it to the ground in terror. That plant doesn't mess around. I have a strange wish for it to be here, to honour my station with its presence.

*

As always, the weekend passes, Monday comes too soon, and I'm back at my station, waiting. I have a hot coffee from a franchise outlet in hand. I'm one red stamp away from a freebie; tomorrow's treat. A few school kids who must be running late are larking about. A middle-aged woman in what looks like a wig rolls her eyes. Across the tracks, the platforms stay silent.

I board the train, pull the novel I'd bought the day previous out of my backpack and sip my scalding coffee. I look out of the smudged glass at my dead platform, the buddleia swaying a little in the breeze. There's a man standing there, waiting. I look at him. He's in his mid-fifties, I would guess; hair with a carbon-date of somewhere around 1982, a shabby suit that has a touch of the official to it. He stands there politely, neither smiling nor frowning, his gaze somewhere in the middle distance. An insistent burst of grass forces its way up through a crack in the platform by his left foot. Face up at the window, I try and see if in his hands he holds keys, a clipboard, a notebook or some kind of surveying equipment to justify his presence. But no, he simply holds his hands together and rocks gently back and forth on his heels. I see his lips purse as he begins to whistle the tune of a forgotten pop song.

The train pulls away. I watch the man, still rocking on his heels, until he's out of sight. I debate whether to jump off at the nest stop, head straight back, somehow break onto the platform and interrogate this interloper. But I have work, and I don't want to be late. I hear the screech of parakeets somewhere high up in the grey sky.

I admire his dedication and know his train will never come.

Gary Budden

XV.
Broken Spectre

It is 1993 and I am in the mountains. It's a part of my job I like. I take boys from difficult homes and broken backgrounds up into the heights of Snowdonia. We travel from the towns and few cities of the south east where the landscape is often flat and woody, or marshy and muddy with imprecise demarcations between land and water. I take the boys in the van farther than many of them have ever been, following the motorways and stopping at the service stations to stock up on sausage rolls and fizzy cans of drink. The cashiers and attendants have accents different to the ones they know and they laugh and mock for the simple fact these people are ever so slightly different. But in some, I see an excitement in the eyes: a challenge but also a possibility.

Over the border, they laugh at the bilingual signs, saying that's not a language, it can't be. They look at the spreading greenery and the off-white dots of sheep covering the fields with scat. I point out floating ravens and buzzards. My colleagues and I keep a sort of order, encourage them and even help with the erection of tents. I laugh off the complaints at the shock of the rain and the mud, the grass that stains denim as they kneel and slide poles through canvas. The idea, I suppose, is to show them something different and to show them what they can do. To make men out of them, some say, but I do not.

We begin the ascent of Cadair Idris early. It's summer but it is cold. Droplets of dew cling in my beard. Bags are packed with fleeces and water. We've kitted the boys out with good walking shoes and a professional guide is with us and I hope all of this will do some good. Hope that wherever life takes them they'll remember this trip in some small way. We climb and I point out cwms, striated rock and moraines. I think I see a lonely red kite.

Today is misty, the sun trying to make inroads through the damp air. The guide leads the procession and I take the rear, ensuring no stragglers fall by the wayside. I am sweating and I swig from my water bottle.

I look behind me into the swirling mists, trying to see how high we've climbed, to try and see the land fall away below. A gigantic black figure follows me, his shape blurry and indistinct, rainbow light coiling off him into the mist. I raise my hand in alarm, and so does the black figure: he mirrors my movements in the mist, this spectre of myself, my mountain shadow high up here.

Boys, I shout, come see this.

XVI.
Tonttukirkko

The Troll Church sits forgotten on its island off the coast of Helsinki, a quiet shaded place in the vast archipelago that swarms round the western Baltic coast. Vartiosaari crawls with life in the brief summer months. Blueberry bushes carpet the forest floor, lush and endless. Raspberries form angry red punctuation marks amongst them. Chanterelle mushrooms sprout with abandon from the damp earth. The London middle-classes pay near ten pounds for the luxury of consuming one hundred and fifty grams of the stuff. The facts seem pathetic, unreal here. Clouds of vicious horseflies, mosquitoes, midges, gnats, gadfly form a united front of insect aggression, harassing visitors as they marvel at the pure unblemished white lichen, signals of health and clean air unknown back home.

Adrianna thinks of this place she visited three years ago, a trip abroad to see the homeland of her Finnish friends. It stays with her in searing detail, too real and too defined. She must return, to escape the crumbling reality of the English capital, where she sees defaced monuments to fallen cyclists, ghost bikes stolen by thieves, empty birds' nests fallen onto cracked pavements. A swelling desire to recapture that other time, the emotions she felt when she stood in Tonttukirkko, with warm damp and fungal rot, only insects and the preternatural for company. Exiting Vartiosaari meant a short swim back to their rented dwellings on another, smaller part of the archipelago, through the warm Baltic Sea where arctic terns floated overhead and great crested grebes bobbed on brackish water.

Here in amniotic brine, she could feel the shades, see memories of ondines in the lower depths, the rumblings of an extinct kraken miles below the surface, the water a mirror reflecting all that her life was not. The insect life created a continual throbbing hum, even as the birds feasted on them. They would always win; strength in numbers.

There was nothing for her to get back to, and the future seemed to stretch on without promise. She had forgotten her orders long ago, lost the reason she was out in the world, alive, breathing. Undercover police call this 'mission drift'. Forgetting who you are, why you are doing what you are doing, becoming something that you, at first, merely imitated.

'Always move forward,' as her progressive friends would say. She was yearning for something that existed in an unrecoverable past. Nostalgia was poison, she knew that. The feelings were there regardless.

It's last night's party, the ephemeral sexual encounter, this is what's making her drift off into comedown reveries of The Troll Church, of Jatulintarha, the stone maze, the ice age boulders, the Viking lookout points at the summit of the island where she and her friends stopped, sweaty and humid after filling buckets of raspberries, blueberries, chanterelles, until they realised they were taking more than they needed and stopped to sit on the stones overlooking the archipelago, looking out to Helsinki itself, smoking rolling tobacco, sipping from plastic water bottles, swatting insects from their skin.

They walked an overgrown road crossing the island, built long ago by Chinese prisoners of the Tsar, fortification workers aiding the defence of St Petersburg during the First World War. All but forgotten and fallen down a crack in history.

No contact with the digital world in over a week and her mind adjusted accordingly. Sitting under swaying trees, looking out across the rippling water at night with her friends, voyeurs to the march of the seasons, animal rituals older than her entire species, the red wine and marijuana, the devouring of her book of feminist science-fiction. Things inside her settled, calmed. 'I feel fucking Zen!' she exclaimed with a laugh.

On Vartiosaari she stayed at The Troll Church whilst her companions climbed higher up the rocky cliff, now twenty metres above sea level, where before it had been touched by lapping waves four thousand years ago. She stood there, savouring the experience. She lies on her sofa, nauseous, and allows herself to be back in the moment. Despite the presence of the crude wooden cross attached to the ancient rock, this is a pagan place, it exists in a world different to the one that she knows and battles with in her day-to-day life. The vegetation becomes lush and the birdsong disappears, the stink of humus and fungus, of fresh new growths bursting from leaf litter all stronger now, and she sees, really *sees* Tonttukirkko, a gathering place at equinox and solstice, tusked masculine bipeds, polyamorous fauns, iridescent plant-men shimmering in shades of emerald, opal and malachite, shambling furry things of giant size that she may once have called trolls, impossibly lithe, woody females indulging in an orgiastic bacchanalia who whisper invitations to her in archaic tongues. Primal creatures, Earth-things that dance and revel, drink and fornicate. A Troupe of Fools, scarred harlequins and grimacing jesters. She sees a narwhal pod out to sea, breaking the surface in clouds of vapour. The trees shudder and sway, their intentions opaque. The ground is a fluid nest of worms, shifting, buckling. A chance of falling, of being swallowed, crushed underfoot by the revellers. Tonttukirkko is alive.

The shouts of her companions from the cliff-top bring her back. It is gone, evaporated. She shakes her head, blinking hard. She joins her companions, who give her odd looks, though this is soon forgotten as she regains her composure, seeming now even more invigorated by the place, by the island, and, as she sits with them on the Viking lookout, staring out across the waters and the dotted islands, she thinks of what she's seen. She smiles, though she mentions it to no one. She thinks of sentries looking out on a guardian island, igniting giant bonfires at the sight of unfamiliar ships, alerting the mainlanders against danger. She tries to picture who these people were, what they hoped for and dreamed of.

Her future is opaque, her skin is becoming translucent, and the past is bottoming out.

Adrianna lies on her sofa, nauseous, her throat sore from coughing. Her body still retains feeling of last night's brief passion. Re-runs of poorly executed American sitcoms flicker on the television, the volume down low. Traffic rumbles outside. A mother shouts at her children somewhere out on the street.

She sips her tea, and wishes she was somewhere else.

XVII.
Spearbird

The bridled was always my favourite, a white ring and slashed stripe giving the bird a bookish air: wise, like it was privy to some essential truth. In late spring and early summer, the breeding months, I see the guillemots giving indecipherable lessons up there on the sheer cliff-face to their tottering young.

The bridled is not a sub-species, just a variation on a theme. The female lays just one mottled egg, conical, resting upon a ledge high up above crashing waves. The loomeries are such a sight.

The bridled guillemot, my favourite living bird.

Scientific opinion, what I've read in my yellowing books and brought up online, says the spearbird too mated for life like its smaller cousins. A solitary egg; no replacement if the first was lost, not until the seasons ran through their cycle. The old maritime stories and seafarer tales say you could see the adults floating, boat-like, their children perched on their backs.

*

I take Denny and Bill, as I do every morning, for a long walk, past my neighbour's house displaying a tasteful blue plaque like the ones you see everywhere in certain parts of London. Marcel Duchamp stayed here, once, just over a century ago ('I am not dead / I am in Herne Bay'). Simon loves this fact, loves that quote, says that's how he felt growing up here.

My circuit takes me along the street, off Mickleburgh Hill, holding the straining Jack Russells back as we cross Beltinge Road leading into the town centre, then onto green slopes that curve leisurely down to the Thames Estuary. Late spring sunshine sparkles on the water and I can see container ships out near the horizon. The blue-bronze statue of Barnes Wallis, who bounced his prototype bombs up the coast at Reculver, stares out to sea. A solitary herring gull perches on his head, mottling his shoulders with shit.

I let the dogs off the lead and throw them a chewed tennis ball. They bound off, fetch it back to drop at my feet. It's soaked with drool and falling apart. We repeat this process as we work our way down to the seafront, stepping off grass onto concrete and walking in the direction of Reculver. The towers are a lonely landmark. But today I can't see them very well; there's a haze in the air, an intimation of summer making the towers a blur and the sandstone cliffs an orangey smudge. Out on the horizon where container ships and Thames barges glide, the Maunsell forts dream of war and the white wind-turbines spin slowly. I walk a good mile along the front until Denny and Bill start to tire, then take the steep path up through the Herne Bay downs, the dogs bounding through cow parsley and nettles, disturbing dunnocks and sparrows. These common birds are part of my daily ritual, providing a necessary rhythm and repetition that helps fill Maggie's absence. We do get surprises here in Kent though. Don't be fooled. A whitethroat. A rust-coloured butcherbird, its larder stocked with large insects and small mammals impaled on sharp thorn. I keep notes of all unusual reported sightings. A little auk spotted down in Dungeness (I imagine it in the shadow of the nuclear reactor). A black guillemot far from home, spotted near Reculver towers.

It's still early and only a few other dog walkers and joggers are about. Just how I like it. I've been walking these routes for forty years now, seen so much change and so much stay the same. At the top of the downs, on a bench I had dedicated to Maggie (*She loved this spot*), sits a sad-looking and stubbled man swigging from a can of something obscured in brown paper.

Was the spearbird ever knocked off course and washed up on this shore?

They say, once, you could see whales off this coast.

*

I've only just got in with Denny and Bill when the doorbell rings. They go mad as they always do, yelping and jumping about excitedly, as if this has never happened before.

I go to open the door. 'Down Denny, down Bill. It's just Simon,' I say, 'just Simon and Ade.' I feel silly still in my walking boots, dry mud flaking off onto the carpet, my outdoor coat military-green and still buttoned up.

'Hello Dad,' he says before I've even fully opened the door. My son, thirty-six years old and back in Kent after a decade and a half in the metropolis. I see my Maggie in him.

'You off out?' he asks with a wink, looking at my boots and coat and ruffling the back of Denny's neck, who growls contentedly.

'Just got in with the dogs,' I say, and it feels weak, but Adrianna, Simon's partner, beams and says, 'Hello Gerry, you alright?' And I feel that I am.

'I'll put the kettle on,' I say.
She's cut her hair. I like her.

*

I've seen black guillemots in their natural habitat, sooty pigeon-sized cousins of the spearbird with lipstick-red feet. They're Celtic birds to my mind, nesters in Ireland, the west coast of Scotland, the Orkneys and Shetland. I've never seen any in England, never knew if that Reculver sighting was correct. When I saw them myself, it was many summers ago on the Isle of Man, when Simon was still little. One of the trips we used to take. They seemed so regular and then they just stopped. I struggle to remember the last trip we all took, together. I remember feeling, there on the island, like a family. Dad, mum, son. Egg mayonnaise sandwiches wrapped in cling-film, sweet thermos tea, and a creased RSPB guide.

It's a strangely quiet bird, the black guillemot. Simon says he can still remember that trip, asking where the manx cats kept their tails. I remember a local fisherman saying something to me in his language and laughing.

Simon doesn't visit as much as I'd like, but he's getting better as we both get older, and I enjoy dusting off the photo album. Now he's moved back to Kent I've seen him more in three months than I have in the last five years.

*

Simon and Ade are early. April is ending, with the first few days of real warmth making themselves known, the world waking up from an endless winter of floodwater and apocalyptic predictions. Showers, spreading greenery, early hay fever sneezes, a slight sweat when I take my walks still kitted out in my winter gear. Yesterday

I saw my first swallow of the year and jotted the sighting down in my notebook. Date, time, location. I would have remembered, but it feels important to document these things.

I pour boiling water over instant coffee, black and sugarless for all three of us. Maggie always insisted on buying the good stuff, boiled it up on the oven the old-fashioned way, refusing both glass cafetieres and the instant supermarket stuff. She ground her own beans. Ahead of her time in that sense, I suppose, but I can't be bothered with all of that if I'm honest.

'Jenny not with you?' I ask Adrianna.

'With her dad,' she says, and sips from her steaming mug. I wish Maggie were here to see her son like this, recovered from a divorce that broke his mother's heart more than his. I wish she were here to see him with someone who makes him happy. He's said to me, privately, after a few whiskies we had on Christmas Eve, this is the first time he's ever felt real happiness. 'I never knew what it meant, until now,' he said. 'And children?' I asked. 'I'm happy to be a step-dad,' was his reply. 'I don't want to create a kid who would have to feel the things I've felt. I hope you understand.'

Maggie's not here. There's only us, and I'm glad they're with me. It's funny, I remember Ade as a teenager. When they were together the first time around in the nineties. Life can blow you off course, yet we can still find our way home.

'Saw my first swallow today, Dad,' says Simon, in a way that feels genuine, more than just making the effort. He's smoking one of those battery-powered things, clouds of sweet smelling apple vapour mingling with the coffee steam. 'Time to try and quit,' he says, and I agree. I smoked myself, for twenty years, but I just can't picture myself doing it now. It gives him a pensive look as he sucks vapour into his lungs.

My cat Sandy comes in through the flap purring. She weaves and winds between Ade's legs. Ade leans down and strokes the cat's guillemot-black fur. She's wearing a frayed top with the sleeves rolled up, multicoloured like a puffin's bill. I go to the cupboard to find some cat food. I can see the bowl's empty.

*

I like razorbills too of course, with their imposing zebra-striped thick-beaks. Aptly named. It'll take a finger off. Closest in look to the spearbird (the bird I dream of, what a sight to see!). You'll find no razorbills on the coast of Kent either. Certainly not in Herne Bay. Simon sometimes asks me why I don't just up sticks and head out to the coast of Wales, Ireland, Scotland, the places I say I really love, and I *do* love them, but my only answer to him is this place is my home. Where I lived with Maggie and where he grew up. Where the bench dedicated to his mother sits staring out over the murky estuary. Where a depressed Duchamp boarded, planning his next move, and where I walk the downs daily with Denny and Bill avoiding teenage cider drinkers, solitary fisherman, too-fast cyclists, nervy dog walkers, couples arm in arm, toddlers yelling at the bruise-coloured sky. This is my home. Roman ruins and wind turbines, retail parks and concrete, oystercatchers and turnstones. My home of forty years. A coast where I can watch the storms galloping in off the horizon. The strange joy of seeing it rain *there* and not here. 'Remember, Simon,' I say, 'I am not dead, I am in Herne Bay.' He always laughs at that. He's moved to the outskirts of Faversham, not too far away. Something must have drawn him back. Maybe it's all just random circumstance but I just don't see the world that way.

I can't live near my guillemots. The auks represent the journey, going somewhere far away and deep inside, familiar but elsewhere. Loading the boot of the car, packing the binoculars and telescope, the travel toothpaste and miniature bottles of shampoo. A sacred place outside my life. I don't want to spoil myself and become bored of the things I love.

I wish I could describe to him my dreams of the spearbird, the great auk. Little-wing, gairfowl, icon of extinction, parallel penguin, bird I will never see.

I wish I could explain my fantasies of orca pods, herds of walrus, the deep north. Visions of ice floes and whaling ships, when a bird bigger and brighter than the guillemot and razorbill flew underwater and nested on Icelandic, Newfoundland, Scottish rock.

I wonder what dreams occupy my son at night.

At South Stack, on my yearly trip, I see puffins. They make me think of the books Maggie and I bought Simon in the '80s. That little black and white mascot, grinning, if a bird could grin. Me in my spectacles like a bridled guillemot, reading him story after story.

I suppose they do look childish, those playful and mischievous burrowing birds. I see the puffins, rainbow bills drooping fry, and I see a hungry caterpillar, a painted tyrannosaur, Reynardine loping in front of a harvest moon, a small boy sat on my knee, the sad-happy memories that flesh out my nostalgia.

Once, I spotted a Brunnich's guillemot, I'm sure, but I was alone and it was never confirmed. I could have called it in on one of the twitcher lines. But I took pleasure in the notion if no one knew but myself, was it ever really there? If a tree falls, and so on. Twitchers are collectors, joyless list compilers, and I don't really understand them.

*

We sit around the coffee table and talk, how Ade's daughter from her first marriage, Jenny, is doing at school, how retirement is treating me, how the festival they both went to in Winchester, months back, went (I'm strangely jealous, I love my music, but the thought of it tires me out). How Simon's new job is going. He's commuting to London two days a week, working from home for the rest. 'Never thought I'd be one of those people,' he says. 'Leaving was like a painful breakup.'

We sit and drink our coffee, a lull in the conversation.

Then Simon says, through clouds of apple vapour, 'Dad, I have an idea. Let's go see your guillemots. South Stack, go with you on your trip. I want to do stuff like that again,' he says, 'take Ade to see it too. I keep telling her about how beautiful parts of Britain can be. She's promised to go just to shut me up.'

'He does keep going on about it,' says Ade, grinning, mischievous like a puffin. I nod, feeling happier than I let show.

'There's choughs there now too,' I say, and my son smiles and drains his coffee. Sandy eats noisily from her bowl.

*

Simon was twelve when I saw little auks fluttering out near the horizon of the Hollow Shore, at least ten of them, starling-sized and in a hurry. It was 1991 on the north Norfolk coast but he says he can't remember clearly. 'A lot of it blends together,' he says. 'It's only now that I'm trying to pick it all apart and stick it all back together again in a way that makes sense.'

He has a way with words, my son.

During that trip we camped in muddy fields, laughed at the rural Norfolk accents, enjoyed the already-ageing rides at Great Yarmouth. We ate plates of heaped meat at Fatty Arbuckles somewhere in the town centre, tired and hungry. A sad place really. I have a photo from that trip of a fallen pillbox, the cliff that held it finally given way to quietly eroding wind and rain. Upside down, half-submerged in the damp sand, cold puddles of salty rainwater pooling in the gloom. It's a fate that will befall

Reculver and my home; but I view the hollow shores I love as a dialogue between land and sea, a conversation I'm not privy to. I don't really believe in endings. Nothing ever ends. There is only change.

I have a picture on my mantelpiece of Simon, my only child, standing on Kodiak Island in a cagoule and chunky boots with pigeon guillemots nesting behind him. After the divorce he travelled a lot. He said it kicked something inside him back to life: all of a sudden he could remember the Isle of Man and the Hollow Shore and South Stack and even bits of north Norfolk. How going away, seeing all these wonderful places in a world he never knew, could be so big, made him see where he was, where he lived in a new light. He took stock and reassessed where he was from. 'I know that's a bit obvious,' he said, 'but it's true.'

I've never seen pigeon guillemots. I've rarely travelled outside of Europe and now I'm getting too old even if I had the urge. My son says I should visit a few more places before time runs out, he'll even go with me, see those birds I only know from books and Attenborough and my magazines. The ones we always fantasised about going to see, chatting away in the car, back in the nineties. The picture is enough for me, I say. And at night I have the spearbird.

One of those magazines, dated May 1995, is stained a deep red from wine Maggie spilled one Christmas. I never threw it out. It's still perfectly readable. Its cover features a striking photograph of a razorbill.

I'm ageing. Every night is a night of nineteenth century dreams. I am on Deadman's Island and I hunt down the great auk, the king of them all, giant flightless father to both guillemot and razorbill. I'm keen for its down: stuffing for my pillow on which to rest my hunt-tired head, hungry for the meat and feather that earns me my living. I taste its flesh, cooked over sputtering flame, rich and gamey. In the petrified ruins of Neolithic fires, they will find the spearbird's remains. Gnawed bones, bits of wing, beaks used in long forgotten ceremonies by the Sons of Cain.

How we project onto the natural world. I love the deep north. I visited the Scottish isles a few times, always hoped to see orca but never did. I photographed bullet-fast gannets, floating terns, seals spinning in the brine. I remember a few old fishermen speaking Gaelic as they hauled nets from icy water; lessons out of reach.

In the islands of Scotland, Newfoundland, Iceland, the deep north, my mind wanders. I watch the lunar cycle at Callanish.

I boat to the nesting sites.

I take the eggs.

It is my hands that throttle the life from the final great auk. It is my heel that lands on the last egg. I wake, sweating, heart pounding, thrilled and appalled. I should dream of my wife; but I dream of the spearbird.I own a reproduction of Keulemans' illustration of the great auk up in my study that I try to imagine in life and in motion. Such poetic names there were for this creature; names that crossed from Norse to Basque, from Old Irish to Inuit.

I stayed with Simon in London before his marriage all went wrong. We visited the Horniman Museum, just the two of us. I looked at the sad taxidermy, and there it was, my spearbird, plastic-eyed, blind like Barnes Wallis but seemingly at peace. Only much later did I discover the truth; a facsimile created from the feathers of other birds. Guillemots and razorbills. Afterwards we looked out over the city from Forest Hill, a sweep of landmarks from Battersea, dead even then, all the way to the towers of commerce in the east. Times like that, I admit, I missed London a little.

In Liverpool, they keep the Earl of Derby's great auk egg. Mottled shell on cotton wool, resting forever behind glass in a lacquered wooden box. I saw it, in the nineties, a few months before Maggie spilled her wine.

*

The telly burbles quietly, this year's annual documenting of the spring awakening on the BBC. I flick through a book Simon bought me for my sixty-fifth, the accompanying hardback to an exhibition along the coast in Margate. He says he knows the artist from his life in London, a woman called Helena Williams. I've been to The Gallery, and enjoyed it.

Guillemots crowd the screen while an enthusiastic voiceover tells me reassuring facts I already know about breeding habits, single eggs and precarious ledges, threats to their environment, differences between winter and summer plumage. The negligible difference between bridled and common.

Denny and Bill doze at my feet dreaming their dog dreams. Sandy bats at the screen trying to take down birds hundreds of miles away. I've seen her do this many times but it still makes me laugh. I named her after a folk singer I used to love; where does the time go? Sandy's nearly twelve now, the old girl, and going deaf. She never littered, I had her fixed, for which now I feel a strange guilt.

Simon and Ade stayed most of the morning. He helped me shift some stuff to the dump. We took another walk with the dogs along the downs in the afternoon. I noticed more swallows in the sky.

We made plans for Wales, for Anglesey, for South Stack. For the guillemots.

*

I'm not from Kent; by which I mean I wasn't born here. I spent the first twenty-five years of my life in London, born to parents in a nondescript part of Islington before the chattering classes, vegetarianism and aspirational lifestyles took root. My early childhood days were spent in a city that was slowly licking its wounds, rebuilding after a war that had necessitated the Maunsell forts in the estuary, the bouncing bombs of my shit-stained statue, the pillbox that would be swallowed whole by Norfolk sand. I was born in 1949, a baby boomer, one of the luckiest generations in history, or so I read. Simon has told me too; even shouted it down the phone once.

I was a child in the monochrome fifties. I can't remember the trip with my parents to the Festival of Britain in '51. They always talked about it. Even had a photo, my black and white toddler-self in front of a murky Thames. Later, I'd look at the Southbank and find its brutal concrete unnerving, fascistic in a way nobody wanted to admit. On the Thames, I always loved watching the cormorants, fanning their reptilian wings as they perched on the remains of the first Blackfriars Bridge. I loved the weird anachronisms everywhere in the city. As if we couldn't clean up behind ourselves properly, had got bored halfway through.

In the sixties, I entered adolescence. I remember unease and protests. Not much swinging. Pesticides poisoned peregrines, dropping them from the sky in the name of progress. Back then I would never have described myself as an ornithologist or a birder or even someone with any real interest in nature, though I must have had something inside me, or how else would I be the man I am today? My mother and father, war-shocked city people, neither pushed for nor prevented any interests of mine. I was always grateful for that. My father fought in Burma, always intimated he'd seen worse things that anyone would or could ever know. I think he enjoyed that. I always held the absurd desire to ask what birds he saw in those jungles, craving stories filled with bamboo and junglefowl. I had the sense he felt my generation weak for not having suffered sufficiently.

Maggie was a year younger than me. I met her in the approach to my twenty-first birthday, 1970, such ancient history. I was listening to folk rock LPs and so was she and I suppose I must have offered to buy her a drink in our local pub. She was a friend of a friend and, what can I say, we hit it off, we fell in love in the way that people used to. Her family *were* from Kent, and we visited them down on the coast, and it was there that I saw oystercatchers skimming in over the water at dusk, Maggie's hand in mine, the sun a bloody orange. I listened to the water lap at the splintery groynes at Seasalter and watched the oystercatchers land. Soon after, I bought my first bird book in a charity shop in Canterbury, and though I'm not sure Maggie ever understood it all in quite the way I did, I think she was happy I had an interest, a hobby, even though I must have infuriated her at times. 'At least you're not one of those football thugs,' she said with a smile. And that interest, my beloved guillemots and choughs and puffins, it took us all around the country and we got to know, really know, the place we lived in, and I loved her for the fact she came with me. Now at night I think of her but I dream of the spearbird.

Maggie always said she thought it was attractive and almost exotic that I was a Londoner, born and bred, and I told her that I felt the same way about her being from the coast, given the opportunity to have some peace and quiet after a life of city streets and bomb craters. London was depopulating rapidly when we met, flights out to the new towns, better housing and perceived better qualities of life, Londoners fleeing into Essex, to Milton Keynes, and many like us, into Kent. She was a returnee, me the immigrant. We left London in 1974. 'I can't believe you left before punk!' Simon says. 'It was never my thing, really,' I say. He rolls his eyes at this, incredulous that I was never as angry as him.

Maybe I was lucky.

Simon wasn't born until 1979. We went through five years of trying and a miscarriage that nearly broke us. I remember days in '77 when Maggie would sit at home with her sisters and they would talk and talk and console and I felt I was intruding somehow, so I'd take solitary walks along the downs with the binoculars that I still own (vintage, I suppose) looking out at a horizon punctuated by the Maunsell forts, yes, and Reculver too, but many years before the turbines would split opinions along this fretful coastline. In those days she was so sad, and seemed so small, and I just didn't have the words. I walked the coast until my feet blistered, drove south into the Romney Marsh, crunched over shingle and looked for crossbills on the Dungeness reserve. I left early in the mornings when Maggie was with her mum to walk the Blean Forest paths. I watched the birds, and it helped, it really did. Gave me a sense I could deal with it all. Gave me the strength to be there for my wife. We headed through the winter of discontent towards the eighties and Simon came along. The only one I want, said Maggie, I just couldn't go through with all that again. She was right, she couldn't, and neither could I.

*

After I take the dogs for their walk I take a wander into town following the seafront. It's a Monday and quiet. I pass Barnes Wallis, gull shit piling up on his shoulders. I get a text from Simon: *Looking forward to the weekend Dad! Glad we're doing this.*

Friday we'll set off for South Stack. I'm heading into town to get a few things: a new pair of decent boots, perhaps get a late breakfast in the Beano café.

'Out of the way granddad!!' Laughter. A few teenagers on skateboards and BMXs speed past me, caps rustling in the wind, rushing toward the arcades and the pier. I sigh.

*

We've crossed the border into Wales. Simon drives as Jenny dozes in the back seat, a Puffin book clutched in her hand. Adrianna sits next to her daughter dozing also, hands resting on her lap. I sit next to my son. Once it was me in the driver's seat. He looks so like his mother. One of Simon's reggae compilations leaks quietly from the speakers. Not my kind of music but I say nothing.

He begins to talk.

'Do you think about Mum? It's three years already.'

'I know, Son. Every day.'

'Do you get lonely?'

'Sometimes. But I'm happy on my own. I'm glad you came home, you know.'

'I am too. When was the last time we did this? I remember being on that back seat, you and Mum in the front. But I can't remember when the last time we did it was. It was in the nineties. I can't believe how long ago it all feels.'

'It's certainly been a while.'

'I need to add some new memories to it all, you know? It's hard to put into words, I just really wanted to come back, with Ade and Jen. Just describing it doesn't do it justice, does it?'

'No it doesn't. I know what you mean.'

'Now we're back, now I'm near you, I want to try and do more of these kinda things, if you do?'

'I'd like that a lot.'

*

We're at South Stack among groups of other birders, telescope tripods hung over their shoulders like the carcasses of a fresh kill, earnest men with beards and bulging bellies, with patient wives who sip tea from plastic containers. The cliffs are teeming, the whir of wings everywhere, life so abundant it seems nearly impossible and, in this moment, everything seems OK.

We set up a good spot, my tripod wedged into the earth and telescope set up. Jenny peers through a miniature set of binoculars and points, tugs my sleeves and asks, 'Uncle Gerry, what's that?' She points at buzzing wings and a rainbow bill.

'That's a puffin, Jen, just like on your books.' She giggles.

There's not an inch of space wasted. This bird city, every possible ledge, crevice and cranny occupied by puffins, razorbills and guillemots. I spy a waddling pair of bridleds, guide Jenny's gaze to them, and she asks why they're wearing glasses, and it's my turn to laugh. Ade and Simon are talking a few feet away from us. I think he's talking about Maggie but I can't quite hear. They're holding hands. Then he grabs his binoculars suddenly, a childish happiness gripping him, says, 'Look look, choughs!' And we all see them, their pointed beaks deep crimson and feathers coal black, something once gone that now is not.

I train my telescope on the loomeries. Down near where sea meets cliff, I see it. That white spot under the eye. The useless wings.

The parallel penguin of my deep north, it's found me after so long.

My great auk, my gairfowl. It startles and dives beneath the waves.

Little-wing.

Spearbird.

Nothing ever ends.

Gary Budden

XVIII.
Wooden Spoons

When I was a little girl, living with Mum and Dad in the town by the creek, my uncle Geoff and his wife Alida lived in a little village, some six miles out in the countryside. I haven't been there in many years. It was always damp but never raining, with lush greenery, dripping beech and ash branches, rolling hills in the distance, set apart and rural in a way I know can only be the fantasy of my metropolitan life.

Geoff was Mum's younger brother. They'd both grown up in the exhaust filled air of the North Circular. Mum and Dad wanted something different and eventually left the grimy pebble-dashed buildings, heading south east to what became the family home. Geoff and Alida (strangely, I never knew how they'd met) decided to follow. She was Dutch, from somewhere near the border with Germany. Her father, people hinted, had been in the resistance, during the long war. They swapped outer-London living to set up home in a place it would now be fashionable to describe as 'tumbledown'.

We'd visit at weekends. Mum and Alida were, to all intents and purposes, best friends. In their cottage were two giant wooden pieces of cutlery, hanging on the wall near the stove. A spoon, a foot long, and a fork to match.

A wooden knife would be no good, I realise now, but back then I wondered about its absence.

'Those are the giant's fork and the giant's spoon,' Alida would say, deadly serious.

Wide-eyed, I would ask where he (I assumed the giant was a he) lived.

'He lives up there in the woods on the hills and eats naughty children.'

'With that fork and that spoon?'

Alida would nod.

I remember that village and the cottage, my uncle and aunt sat with Mum and Dad around a splintery wooden table, drinking tea or maybe coffee, smoking Drum tobacco brought in duty free on the ferries from Holland. I would watch and listen to the adults and try to make sense of what they said, place names that I had no memory of like Horsenden Hill and Wembley Stadium.

Alida had a series of books, kids' books, though back then they had no children, my cousins somewhere still in the future. The books were all in Dutch, except one that I remember was in German.

The illustrations had that kind of Old World European quality, a style that I can only describe as melancholic and faded, even back then set in the unrecoverable past. Gnomes and woodland beings and straw revenants, doing whatever they do – I could read by then, but, of course, could not read the Dutch. One image still stands out of a huge being, made from water and mist, striding with purpose far out to sea as a tiny couple watch from a hollow shore.

I imagined the adults were discussing the beings who stalked the weald and the low hills of the Kent countryside; if only I could see them. The books and the wooden cutlery fascinated me, gave me fretful dreams, thrills and anxieties as I walked the woods and marshes of my childhood.

Now I am older, having wrung out of my London life all that I can, I still hope one day to stumble across a giant footprint, perhaps flooded with water and home to pond skaters and water boatmen. I wonder what happened to that wooden spoon and fork, and wonder still why Alida had them.

I still see Geoff and Alida from time to time – they are family after all – even though they've been divorced going on seven years now. I always want to ask about that hanging carved cutlery and the giants, but I never find the right moment.

Gary Budden

XIX.
Our Own Archipelago

Two days since Midsummer passed. We partied all night on the decking of the summer cottage. We drank strong beer with a bear's face snarling back at us from the tin, then sweated it all out in a sauna that smelled of birch. When the heat got too much we dived into the chilly sea, our blood racing and hearts pumping. We repeated this process until we collapsed on sofas and futons and floors, our skins pink and new, the sun never truly dipping below the horizon. At best, it was a purple crimson glow around 4 a.m., a clean comedown light. After our conversations were put to bed, the only noise was the splash of mating grebes out on the water and the tremolo of passing oystercatchers.

The morning after, Edla and I said goodbye and left for the archipelago.

*

'I can't really talk right now, Elliott, I'm on holiday, you know that. I came to get away from all this for a while.'

'He's bad and getting worse. I think we need to talk about care. A home or something.'

'Okay. Okay. Can we speak when I get back?'

'Okay. I'm just worried, you know?'

'I know.'

My brother hangs up and I pinch the bridge of my nose.

*

I stand on the rocks, looking out over the waves in a borrowed fleece that smells of winter storage and old tobacco. The wellingtons Edla has lent me are a lurid crimson with floral patterning: child's boots from her summer holidays here long ago, boots that barely fit. The rubber bites hard and I wiggle the toes of my right foot to fight off pins and needles, stamp down onto the hard stone to keep the blood flowing. Clear brackish water breaks gently on a pebbly shore.

It's wet here; the rain, of course, but there's an all-pervading dampness in the air I breathe. It lays trapped in the bulbous mosses and silent sphagnum that carpet the island. Everything is lush and green and damp. I can hear the creaking of wood and my own breathing is too loud in this place. I hear a tiny splash, like a coin dropped in an ornamental pond. An arctic tern, snow-white and jet-black with a blood-red bill, climbs into the air, two small fish hanging from its beak.

I thumb in the pocket of my borrowed fleece and dig out my phone. The one bar of reception is hesitant. I promised myself I wouldn't use it, but the situation, well, it's hard to switch off from the world, as much as I need to. I look at the last text from Elliott, all lists of instructions and what-ifs and what-to-dos about Dad. I know he's right, that he can't live on his own anymore. I don't know what to do. I watch the tern dive again, picturing the word 'orphan' emblazoned in crimson letters on a giant billboard.

I put the phone back in my pocket, the text unanswered. I have the awful knowledge that this scenario, it's nothing new, is happening to a thousand other families right now, has happened a thousand times before and will continue to happen for as long as there is sun in the sky. As long as people celebrate solstice and Midsummer, shit like this will be happening. I can't decide if that makes it all better or indescribably worse. It's absurd, unfair, selfish, but my dilemma is just another cliché. Like we all get trapped in roles that we never even wanted.

Over there, somewhere, is Sweden. I squint and try and make out a landmass but can't tell if what I see is simply wishful thinking. Is it yet another island of the archipelago?

We rowed to the island this morning, my arms aching and a hand punctured with splinters from the ageing oars. In the city, I have no opportunity to do things like this and I resent that. I look admiringly at the angry blister forming on the inside of my right thumb. It'll leave a scar, and I'm glad. It's the mark of something having happened. You could see scars as a sign of trauma – or a record of having lived and survived. My city hands are only good for thumbing messages on my phone and obligingly clicking a mouse at work. Here, they're put to use. I will look at this scar in the future and think: I was there, and I did that.

Edla drove the sixty or so miles from the rented summerhouse where we'd partied with our friends. An hour and a half of torrential rain, the road signs bleeding from Finnish into Swedish, the Swedish words easier to comprehend for an English speaker, the Finnish ones stuffed with 'k's and as long as your arm.

On the drive we stopped for petrol. Standing on the roadside verge were badly made statues of grinning goblins and an inquisitive moose with a distended nose, made from what looked like lacquered papier-mâché. I took a photo.

I watch the arctic terns glide through the air. I think of the solstice celebrations back home that I always wanted to be a part of but never was. Dad always liked that stuff, visited those kinds of places with Elliott. I was Mum's girl, never interested. Or I was told girls should not be interested in such things. I can't remember. Now I'm keen to do this stuff and he's no longer there, not really. It's hard to see him slipping away. When the mind starts getting carpet-bombed by dementia, where does the self go?

I've never seen the sun set at Stonehenge, or sat surrounded by the stones at Avebury. It seems so much easier to take part in someone else's customs, to be the tourist. You're removed from the problems and politics and contradictions that way. This, I promise myself, must change. I throw a mottled grey pebble into the water and listen to its splash. I head back to the cabin.

Inside the fire crackles and pops, eating up splintery logs and bits of balled-up newspaper printed with out of date Swedish headlines. I sip the whisky Edla hands me and pull the wellingtons off my feet. It burns my throat. I stare out of the window at the clear sea, the light dimming slightly, though I know darkness here is an impossibility.

After a while, the fire begins to wane. I volunteer to head to the wobbly stockpile in a mildewed and dust-coated shed, set away from the summerhouse. A rusted hoe and a recently-used garden fork stand propped against one wall. I fill up a wicker basket with chopped logs whose bark flakes off in dusty spurts and walk slowly through the wetness back to the cabin. I smile at the carved greeting that hangs by the door, a mallard stamped with the word 'Valkommen!'.

Edla pours more drink as I place logs on the fire. She's spread out dark rye bread and a kind of pickle spread you squeeze from the tube-like toothpaste. Some pickled herring and local smoked salmon, the colour of St Pancras station. The taste is unbelievable. The fire, the whisky and the quiet: this is the kind of place where you're *supposed* to unburden yourself to a trusted confidant. So I talk a little about Dad, about one of his confused angry flare-ups, the smashed wine glass, the small shards and the dotted beads of bright red on my calf like a gory archipelago: his jumbled apologies and my faith in him retreating like the outgoing tide. I knew it wasn't his fault, exactly.

It's hard to vocalise these things, the words fleshing out the situation, putting meat on its bones. Talking to Edla, it becomes this living, breathing thing that can't be ignored.

'He needs proper care,' she says quietly. I place a slice of salmon in my mouth and chew, thinking.

Edla drains her glass, changes the subject by tapping the window and gesturing outside.

'Tove Jansson lived on an island near here.'

I nod but she can see I don't know what she means.

'Moomins.'

And I giggle like a kid, choking slightly on my whisky, picturing dumpy hippo-things somewhere out there on the archipelago.

It's odd to be sitting here, in the childhood retreat of my best friend. We met at university in Brighton. A long time ago now, a different life spent punching the air at left-wing gigs and smoking Golden Virginia on trips to the Hollow Shore. I miss the English Channel and the burnt skeleton of the West Pier. We went our separate ways, but even when I haven't seen her for half a year it feels as if no time has passed. And these days we have our instant messaging, the free video calls on our laptops. The endless ways to stay in touch, things I once thought of only in terms of science-fiction.

Our conversations are never a struggle, silences never awkward. As I grow older, I realise that finding someone who really understands what you're talking about is a rarity. It's something to hold on to. I never had it with Mum, Elliott, with Dad.

Edla's face is flushed with the fire's heat and alcohol. 'The island over there,' she says, pointing out of the window toward one of the neighbouring islands, 'once, my grandparents were here for summer with the family. They did it every summer. One evening they were just sitting down to dinner, and they see these things come out of the forest. Moose. A family of moose who needed to get from one island to the other, they'd got stranded somehow. My grandpa would always tell that story of the family of moose swimming from one island to the other. They don't like to swim normally. It feels like I saw it myself.'

I think of huge papier-mâché beasts disintegrating in the water. Before I can reply, a mobile starts buzzing. I listen to Edla speak in rapid-fire Swedish to her grandmother, letting her know that we made it to the island OK, that we have enough logs on the fire and that we're eating well. Edla's grandmother is eighty-seven and has lived in the area all her life. She heard the rumble of Russian guns during World War Two and her husband died long ago. She speaks no word of Finnish and yet here we are, in Finland. I try to imagine what Dad would think of those animals crossing the archipelago and the muffled boom of a war too close for comfort.

I've let the battery run down on my mobile.

*

'When I was a little child,' says Edla, handing me a thermos, 'I was sitting right here on these rocks like we are now.' I sip hot coffee and look at the distant islands. 'I was maybe six. So, this is in the eighties of course. And I see something come up out of the water and I run in to tell Grandma and Grandpa that I've seen a whale! And Grandma she scolds and says, "silly Edla there is no whales here," and I say no but Grandma come look look! And she looks, and she sees what I saw but it was not a whale. You know what it was?'

I'm curious. 'What?'

'A Russian submarine. Cold War. It shouldn't have been there and there it was.'

I have the absurd image of a sub rising by a burnt Brighton pier.

I say, 'At Midsummer, I was sitting next to Tuomas out on the pier and he was just scribbling in a notebook. I ask him what he's writing and he says, with not a hint of humour, "I try and write down my dreams. I had a dream I was the only one left alive on an island and the invading army were coming and I knew I was going to die. The army, I knew, were the Russians."'

'A very Finnish nightmare!' laughs Edla.

I don't tell her about the boozy sauna kiss we shared, his smile as I poured water onto hot coals and the smell of birch heavy in the air.

*

It's as dark as it's going to get and the sky is a bruised plum colour. I've hauled on my wellingtons to head to the outhouse. I've put it off for long enough. Dad always enjoyed the outdoor life; Mum was mortified at the thought of pissing in anything that she couldn't flush. I walk down the rough path, careful not to slip on the damp moss. By the outhouse, in the undergrowth, I hear a rustling and see the shuffle of a furry animal disrupting the peace. It waddles out in front of me. It looks like a raccoon, marbled dark brown and creamy white fur, and reminds me of a giant stocky pine marten. It snuffles around for a bit like the hedgehogs used to do back home in Mum's garden, before the illness took her. It disappears off into the purple haze. Does it live here, or swim between the islands?

I am not sure what I have seen.

*

'Look, Elliott, I don't know, I really don't.' Finally, I've buckled, recharged the phone and am taking one of my brother's calls. I'm in the kitchen. His voice is crackly and breaking up.

'What am I supposed to do? I can't just up and leave my job, leave London. He needs proper help. We're not qualified.' Though, as I say it, the thought of evacuating the city through circumstance rather than choice has a real appeal.

'I know, I know,' he says. He sounds tired. I can hear Edla laying the table in the other room and humming some Swedish song tunelessly to herself. She said to me the other night, 'The best way to guess what someone's going to do is look at what they've already done.' I examine a chipped mug. Papa Moomin stares back at me.

I say, 'Look, I just don't know. Talk when I'm back. I'll come down and see you both. Okay?'

Hanging on a hook in the kitchen is some old tourist tea towel. *London's Open Spaces*. Cartoonish illustrations of Hyde Park, Kensington Gardens and Leicester Square. My gut churns at the thought of returning.

'I'll speak to you when I get back, Elliott.'

And I hang up.

*

Edla's family own half of the island. Another family use the eastern half for their own gatherings. After we've eaten, we head out for a walk around the circumference of the island. The other family are absent. It's just the two of us. As we walk, I get a real sense of how this tiny island in this deserted archipelago feels like a country in miniature. We clamber over the huge rocks at the shoreline, almost slipping on green-black seaweed. Fallen branches crack beneath our feet, as loud as gunshot in the silence, as we head through a patch of trees. I hear a scratching above me. A red squirrel high up in an evergreen. Then the ground softens, becomes marshy, making me think fondly of the salt-marshes of the Hollow Shore where I grew up and where Dad still lives. Finally we reach the other summerhouse. Signs of recent life are dotted about. The remains of a children's party among the trees, a few lurid burst balloons lying limp on the lichen, silver streamers tied to twigs and fluttering in the wind.

Clearly the family spent their own Midsummer celebration out here. I feel like I'm in a rural horror film from the 1970s or a C.L. Nolan story. Near the waterline, I find an offering left to appease something or someone, like a Christian cross spliced with the Green Man. It's held in place with near-invisible wires that I stumble over as I approach.

Perhaps inspired by this melancholy scene, Edla says, 'Two years ago, there was a murder near here. No crime ever happens so it was a big deal. Some lady, a biologist for the trees I think, she set up home here. One of the older men in the area, a lonely man, he becomes in love with her, she does not love him back, and he shoots her out in the woods. Very sad.'

I wonder why she's telling me this.

It takes a good forty-five minutes to circle the island. I point out a nesting grebe obscured by yellow reeds. We pass a boat covered with a mildewed and mouldy tarp.

My phone is back in the cabin.

*

My arms are aching pleasantly. I can feel the wooden oar chafe against my blister, now plastered over but still smarting. Edla hangs off the side of the boat, her camera slung low around her neck, looking like a mid-twentieth-century anthropologist. We edge away from our island, Edla snapping away at whatever takes her fancy. I focus on navigating past a clump of barely submerged rocks, the tips of green reeds brushing against my arms and face. The sky is a dull blue, the sun lurking behind sullen cloud.

An oversized gull watches us from a rocky outcrop. Further out on the water is a solitary swan with a banana-yellow beak, bobbing on the gentle waves. It's different to the ones on the canals back home, but I don't know the right name for it. 'Swan' suddenly doesn't seem good enough.

I row for a long time. My shoulders throb and I feel hot blood flow through me. Cold spray hits my face. I look at Edla, her buttoned up jacket the colour of white lichen. She's attempting to photograph the unknowable swan but it's too far away for her lens. The only sounds the click of the camera, the slap of oars on water and the low sighing of the wind.

The only other people I've seen are buzzing on a motorboat far out towards the horizon. The noise was an intrusion, the boat's wake a boiling scar.

Slowly, as we head toward Yttergrund, the lighthouse comes into view, red and white like a lifebuoy. I lose rhythm slightly as I stare at the isolated tower, one of my oars slapping the water like a useless withered limb. In this landscape, the lighthouse feels imposed, the centrepiece of a post-Soviet science fantasy.

Edla lowers her camera, squints at me, and speaks loudly over the wind, 'The lighthouse is empty now. The lighthouse keeper, he was an alcoholic, a drunk, and he falls to his death one day, from the lighthouse, and since then out of respect, I think, no one uses the lighthouse. He has no wife, no family. I don't think it is needed anyway. The lighthouse I mean.'

I nod and think of the solitary motorboat.

I begin to row again, keen now to get to this bigger island and its ghosts.

'Edla,' I ask, spray entering my mouth, 'do you ever get orca around here?'

'I think not, no.' And she shakes her head solemnly. I'm disappointed, but her apologetic expression makes me laugh.

We reach our destination, hitting land and hauling the boat up onto the bank, tying wet rope around a tree, emptying the boat of water with a small plastic scoop. I look at a damp and mildewed information sign welcoming us to Yttergrund, with a green map of the island dotted with points of interest: a few wooden red cabins, a windmill, and the lighthouse oversized and majestic, stretching into the sky.

We start walking. If our island is a country then this is a lonely continent. I stop to look at the illustrated sign by a WC building. A smiling seal that resembles a jolly fat man. A few bees buzz from plant to plant and Edla keeps snapping away with the camera, seemingly at random. The lighthouse remains a constant in our field of vision.

After a while the woods and cabins thin out and we reach the island's other shore. Huge rocks lift out of the water and we clamber up them, jump and shriek like schoolgirls over the gaps between, a tiny taste of daring.

Yellow-green algae grows in small rock-pools, almost fluorescent. Edla heads toward the water's edge in search of more imagery. I sit down, pull out the small pair of binoculars I brought with me and spot two of the yellow-beaked swans floating like showboats on the open water. The buzzing motorboat is now nowhere to be seen. The sky is huge like the skies of the Thames estuary and I feel an odd sensation that's some mix of nostalgia and homesickness, but for a place I've never been and things I've never experienced. I feel tiny and enjoyably insignificant.

On the rocks, we eat our packed lunches, share a cigarette, have a nip of whisky from Edla's hip flask. I ask Edla about the creature I saw by the outhouse.

'The raccoon dogs!' She claps her hands in glee. 'The Russians bred them for fur for their armies. They escaped and went wild. I see them lots on the island. They are from China, originally, I think.'

'Feral, not wild,' I say.

After some time pushing through pine trees, we reach the lighthouse. It's punctured with austere black windows and the red-white metal panelling curves up high above the tree-line. Amongst the woods and the lichen, the smiling seals and brackish algae pools, it resembles an abandoned piece of alien technology, its use opaque. I remember a Russian sci-fi film I saw in my university days and try to picture the lighthouse keeper, drunk and isolated, losing himself in this place. Perhaps sipping spirits by a fire, alone and with only yellow-billed swans for company. That final tumble. Bone on earth. What happens to the self on impact? What do all these experiences add up to? I worry that, in the end, I'll end up as just an anecdote, a story that someone tells to an inquisitive visitor long after I've lost control of my own story. I wonder what Tuomas is doing back at the summerhouse and recall the smell of birch.

It's hard to think soon it will be only me and Elliott, alone in the world, only the two of us to make up that word 'family'.

I pull my phone out, the one bar of reception looking firm. I text my brother: *I'm sorry I've been like this. When I come back, we're going to do what we have to do. We'll get it sorted. It's been hard to take in. I really do care.*

I crane my neck and stare up at the lighthouse. You should see this, Dad. You should see the rainbows rising vertical from far-off islands at five in the morning. Fill your lungs with this air and feel white lichen in your palm. See the giant Soviet subs rise like leviathans. I think you'd like it. You'd have been able to tell me what that swan was, more about the raccoon-dog fur farms, why in this part of the country they all speak Swedish. I'll try and tell you all about it when I get home.

I think of me, my mum, Dad and Elliott, rowing from shore to shore in our own archipelago, laying out wreaths at Midsummer, chopping wood for a fire that would never end, happy and with nowhere else to be. The four of us looking to the lighthouse for guidance. Huddling in our cabins against the winter storms and lashing rain, shelling crayfish in summer, watching moose swim from shore to shore.

I leave tomorrow.

I'm ready.

Gary Budden

XX.
We Are Nothing but Reeds

It's been a hard few weeks in the city. Unseasonably mild, the skies like grey slate, greasy rain sliding down train windows. The crush of commuters always worse in such weather, as if the rain magnifies their numbers.

John and Lucy live together, have done for a few years now, but these few weeks, bar brief bouts of warm embrace in the mornings and a quick dinner at night as they watch Channel 4 sitcoms, they haven't really seen each other. They haven't shared what lifestyle magazines call quality time. Life reduces itself. Home in the flat, brief snatches of respite, early to bed but never a satisfying night's sleep. The same routes every day through the rain and the crushed commuters, to and from office spaces where somehow the hours pass but little seems to change moment to moment. This is work, this is life and this is what grownups do.

Sometimes, John, as the train rattles and shudders, leaves his book open on his lap and watches the others, his fellow

Londoners. People like himself, he supposes. There's the pretty girl in the hijab who he sees every day and who boards at Gospel Oak. There's the bearded white guy with the paint spattered trousers and sunken, angry eyes. Next to him, hunched forward, is the man in the suit frantically playing Candy Crush. Where can they all possibly be going? Maybe they watch him like he watches them. He'll never know. Book open on his lap, he watches these unknowns, and he thinks of being somewhere else, of crashing surf, of footprints in wet sand obliterated by the tides. John is getting headaches and constant lower back pain. Constant screen glare and a life spent sitting. Right eyeball twitching and a daily gulp of painkillers.

Lucy is suffering. Her work, it's important, but dealing with London's lost, with the abused and the hated and forgotten, of course it takes its toll. Lucy had a friend, Lisa, and two years back Lisa fell into the water at Tottenham Lock and never came back up. Lucy feels guilt when she realises she hasn't thought about her.

Her work is, if they admit it, more important than John's. Stress trumps boredom, after all. They try not to raise the subject, know that life, and a relationship especially, should not be a competition. It's a path that leads to only one destination. But she's tired, she needs a break. She is spent at the end of the day, emotions drained, has little left to give. John tries to understand and to keep a respectable distance, but it's hard sometimes. Physical contact has dwindled. This is how it goes, sometimes, right?

The weekends pass in a blur. Maybe a pint on a Friday, a long lie-in come Saturday morning, that brief chance to snatch some sleep back from the world. There are family commitments. Dementia is taking John's dad and his mum needs help. There's guilt at missing social occasions with friends who they once saw all the time, then infrequently, and now almost never. When they do meet, the time goes so fast, too much is drunk and there might be a line of powder to take the edge off. The next day's a write-off, guilt, paranoia and anger at wasting Sunday on the sofa watching reruns of amateur cooking shows. On his train journeys John thinks about all those years he wasted, and spent wasted, all that possibility that seemed within reach at the edge of oblivion. He feels sick to think about it now. Nostalgia also.

Where does all the time go? This is London, for god's sake! There's so much on offer. Only open up a laptop and see all that you're missing. John and Lucy, they take an interest in life and they want to be out at the cinema, the galleries, the gigs, readings and talks. But plans stay theoretical and when they do make it out, one eye is always kept on the time writ large on an iPhone screen. We can't stay too late, they say, we have work in the morning.

Finally the weather is getting colder. John greets this with a kind of relief. The climate, it's not right, it's telling us that something is going wrong. He watches the screeching flocks of green parakeets above Finchley Road and dreams of other lives he could have had – could have still, perhaps.

It's decided on a Tuesday, eating gourmet burgers at the local gastropub. We need a break, let's get away, says John, and Lucy, though so tired, agrees, knows it's important. What is all this for if it's not to be able to go away, *do* something, enjoy a bit of life.

It's off-season. Let's find a cottage somewhere, maybe an Airbnb, somewhere on the coast, an open fire, walks by the cold North Sea. I know a place where you can see *seals*. This is what John says as he sips his overpriced bottle of IPA.

So they do it. Find a small old fishing village on the north Norfolk coast, sort it online with a few clicks, book the train tickets nicely in advance to get a cheap fare, and they look forward to it. It's only a couple of days, but it's a change of scenery and they will be together, for what feels the first time in an age. Away from all this.

The week before they go, Lucy sleeps badly. Her dreams are strafed by guilt that she can retreat, leave, when the people she works with (they call them clients) remain locked inside, movements monitored, trapped in a city that her and John love and hate in equal measure.

Her nan, long dead now, was a Scot, and at night while John snores, she lies awake thinking of those stories Nan would tell, of the seals who were also people. The selkie romances that always ended in tears.

John imagines thick mists rolling in from the North Sea, and in that mist a huge figure silhouetted in the gloom. He grew up by the Hollow Shore, and he couldn't wait to get away, but god, now he misses the sigh of the waves, the smell of salt and the sound of gulls on the roof of his mother's house. Could they ever live back in such a place? What about work, money, what would they do?

The day comes, and they stand at King's Cross under a giant memorial poppy, clutching hot coffee from Café Nero, dragging a squeaky-wheeled suitcase behind them. They board the train, and somewhere in the fields outside of Cambridge they see a pair of muntjac hopping through the crops. I want more of this, thinks Lucy. But to verbalise this would be to admit there might be something wrong, and as yet she cannot do that. John points out a hovering kestrel, and Lucy smiles.

At King's Lynn where the train ends there is bright wintry sun. A cab from there, it's expensive but whatever, this is important. Finally they get to their rented space. It's small and rustic and rural, it has the open fire. It's quiet. There are pictures of hounds and red-coated hunters on the walls. It's that kind of place, John says. Outside the window, a path leading onto the saltmarsh, and beyond that the flat expanses of sand and the North Sea. A small selection of books on an old bookcase. Lucy picks up *We are Nothing but Reeds*, a battered reprint anthology of stories by C.L. Nolan. She flicks through the book, likes the story titles; 'The Sea Giant', 'Mind of Shakan', 'The Cut'. It feels appropriate.

They unpack, and Lucy cracks open the bottle of spirits a friend gifted them after a trip to Finland, and they have a little toast, the clink of glass loud in the silence. It feels good as it warms their stomachs and they get the fire going. They watch light rain drizzle against the windows. They cook a proper meal on the small stove. They get a bit drunk, but it's not the desperate and rushed drinking of their weekends, it feels right and proper. They go up to the small, neat bedroom and for the first time in months they undress and roll around in the sheets and feel at peace.

Afterwards, they lie in bed, the small wall-mounted TV showing Channel 4 news. John clicks on his laptop, leafs through the old guidebook he's brought with him. Finally he says, this is where the seals are, and points to a spot on the map perhaps three miles away, a channel cutting through the sand straight from the North Sea. They can walk there. We'll set off early, they agree.

Morning comes, the cries of oystercatchers, gulls and turnstones seeping in from the marshes. They wake and stretch, brew coffee on the hob, listen to the quiet. As John showers, Lucy reclines in the old armchair in front of the fire and leafs through the introduction to Nolan's book. There's a quote about folklore:

> *'Psychic shrapnel embedded in landscape, letting us enter into a living relationship with the past.'*

They pull on their walking shoes, zip up waterproofs and pack bottles of water. Lucy clutches a camera. John slings binoculars around his neck.

Then they're out of the cottage and onto the creaky wooden path that winds through the brackish marsh. Dog walkers and joggers pass them with a hello or a nod. A few stubborn blackberries still on the bushes. Flocks of migrating geese overhead, the burble of black curlews. Lucy photographs a child's pink glove, now mildewed and lying damp among the reeds.

They reach sand and the coast. They pause at an embossed memorial, dedicated to a young child swept out to sea back in 1994. They walk that bit slower now, heavy prints in the yellow earth. Flatness in all directions and the wind whipping them hard. Look, says Lucy pointing and tugging at John's sleeve. He sees what she sees, far out and sunken in the mudflats, the wreckage of a ship, wooden and colonised by silt. The landscape is treacherous.

This is perfect, says Lucy, her eyes tearing from the wind and her words lost. She photographs driftwood that she imagines will burn blue, the fractal patterns made by razor-clam shells. John peers through binoculars, hoping to spot scoter or eider perhaps. A man and his young child fly a kite.

Eventually the unnamed channel comes into view. We're here, shouts John over the wind.

And suddenly, there are the seals. In this sheltered channel they bob and dive, and one hauls itself from the water, blubbery and ridiculous. Lucy realises why they must take human form. They are water things, not of the world she lives in, and she feels a kind of envy. This is something she will remember.

For a long time, John and Lucy sit on a dune, buffeted by the wind, and watch the seals. A middle-aged man walks past with his dog. Magical things, aren't they? And the couple nod and smile.

Heading back, a mist is coming in off the cold North Sea. It's cold and drops of condensation bead their clothes, John's beard,

Lucy's tied-back hair. The world is hushed in the mist and they are glad they are returning to the cottage.

John looks out to sea. He supposes he should be frightened at what he sees. In the swirling mists, he sees the silhouette of an impossibly huge figure, moving gently and slowly, not hostile or friendly but merely indifferent.

He watches the sea giant go, disappearing in the direction of the wreck.

I'm looking forward to getting the fire going, says Lucy finally. And at those simple words, John feels a burst of feeling for her, so strong it's almost pain. He thinks it might all be okay.

That night they sip more spirits and look out over the marsh as the sun dies for the day. The wind is up and the rushes hiss and whisper. Smoke from John's cigarette hangs blue in the air.

Lucy squeezes John's hand and whispers, perhaps to herself, we are nothing but reeds.

What's that? says John.

Nothing. Doesn't matter.

And she kisses him on the cheek.

Gary Budden

XXI.
The Wrecking Days

It was the magwitching hour; sun like soft gold on the tips of reeds.

– from 'Skydancer', *Stories from the Marsh: The folklore of the Hollow Shore*

The name came later, as we retrofitted chunks of our lives and tied them up with clever titles. We were underachievers with verbal flair, lyrical flourishes and a sharp wit, packaging our time into neat parcels. The wrecking days are, for most of us at least, safely compartmentalised, sitting in a past as unrecoverable as the eroding waterline of a home I haven't visited in years.

Events that fell during the wrecking days, out on the flat marshes of the Hollow Shore, can be safely explained away. I enjoyed the sleep deprivation, my bleary bloodshot eyes watching shore harriers, a bird endemic to the region, coil and pirouette over the reeds at sunrise as Jenny – she called the birds skydancers – lay snoring in my lap, my coat her improvised duvet. Danny smoking thick spliffs and telling us his tales of the overgrown hoverport near his home, the Sons of Cain out on the island, the spearbird his dad swore he saw.

I can still see Helena and Adrianna spinning stones towards empty Stella cans propped on rotting breakwaters. The mud at low tide, exposing lugworm coils and strange detritus laid out in patterns waiting to be decoded.

I miss the wrecking days. I miss the slow ebb of narcotics leaving my body, pissing in the reeds at dawn to the sound of birdlife, buzzing crickets and the strange looped grunt of mating marsh frogs. It was during the wrecking days that I realised the artificial and natural were not different at all. All existed in the world, and all was true.

Back then we were small town kids with underground ambitions, heading for the places where reality thinned and the decadent and divine could be indulged. The only good system was a sound system, we all agreed, and we had better drugs than you. The raves and parties, dancing around crackling fires that turned blue with salt, form the core of the wrecking days. I can't ever forget them.

But years go by. Now, Jenny says I can't let go, that I'm stuck there somehow in the stinking mud, being dragged down below the murky water choking on reedroot and the plastic shit chucked in there by a world that didn't care. What scares me is that I find the thought compelling, and then I think of Danny, screaming in a cell, or on a ward, or wherever he may be.

*

Over the water from the Hollow Shore, across a strip of water called the Swale, lies Deadman's Island. It has a real name somewhere on an OS map, something official printed on paper, but, as Danny was fond of saying, the map is not the territory. The map is wrong – living in London taught me that.

On a clear day and at low tide, you could see the rotted and rusted remains of one of the prison hulks that had gone down in a hazy past. Scuttled or an accident, none of us knew, and historians still speculate about what really happened, as if that matters. But the French bodies that washed up on the Hollow Shore and Deadman's Island joined a soil that already held the bones of their comrades. Grisly relics from the days of Old Boney. Prisoners who'd died on the ships, ravaged by cholera, dysentery, the busy fists of the English. Forgotten bodies in shallow graves, buried beneath the soil of our hollow shores.

So: Deadman's Island.

It made me think of the choose-your-own-adventures I still had copies of. Could imagine a pulp paperback depicting a skeletal soldier rising from the mud, a place of only death and life. During the wrecking days, I would look out at the island and wonder if there was a time when the world was not at war.

Deadman's Island was home to heaving clouds of Brent and Canada geese, scoter and scaup, black-throated divers and occasional sightings of little auk flocks out on the horizon. Danny's old man Fen, birder that he was, claims to have seen a pair of nesting spearbirds on the rocks of the north shore of the island. Impossible, of course, but Fen and Danny alike were bullshitters; it was a family thing, bred in the bone, charismatic and unreliable. The spearbird was extinct, as much a mythology now as the Sons of Cain, bestial half-men that archaeologists claimed to have found evidence of in the island's soil. Those are just the mangled remains of the French prisoners, was the counter-argument, but the Sons are popular folk-devils of the area, grinning not-men that the people of the coastline need more than they could ever admit. The Sons lead a whole host of strange things that were said to have once inhabited the wetlands. Black curlews, white herons. The ghost of a booming bird that resembled a crane. Spearbirds.

And, the straw revenants.

*

The very last time I saw Danny, before he went under (or fucked off, got banged up, topped himself), we sat in a pub in Tottenham, drinking a new fashionable brand of IPA, many years after the wrecking days. Danny had a habit of speaking in soundbites, as if he were quoting choice nuggets from a larger text only he had access to. His eyes were calm, and the strange things he said were like statements of literal fact.

What I mostly remember him saying was, 'Memory is a marsh.'

*

I don't want to paint too rosy picture of the wrecking days. I hope I'm clear headed when I look back. Obviously, there were things that were fucked up and it was irresponsible and dangerous to our health. But I loved it. I may, in the end, have lost a friend, but I met and fell in love with the woman who remains my partner to this day. I saw sunrises that could stop your heart, birds that could snatch the breath from your lungs and carry a loving soul to heaven. I saw things that simply couldn't be.

Some of us can't deal with that, some of us can, and if we can, we deal with it by shutting parts of ourselves down.

Danny couldn't. He said it was because, simply, he saw things too clearly. Like he saw the world for what it really was and that was what was making him come undone.

I imagined my friend seamed and stitched, waiting to be pulled apart, a future unravelling.

So, when we all agreed that the straw revenants could not be real, that we'd fed for too long a diet of cheap speed, indie horror films and C.L. Nolan stories, I knew Danny didn't believe it. He knew he had to try and pass as any other contented inhabitant of the grey towns we grew up in, but I knew the stitched things with faces of dirty sackcloth and bodies of sharp straw were as real to him as the skydancers and marsh frogs.

And what can I say? The Hollow Shore did – does – have a mythic quality to it. There's just something about the place. I feel the pull of the marshes myself and, even now, I find myself walking the cracked concrete and dirty tarmac of Tottenham and imagine boggy ground and sibilant sedge all around me. At weekends, you'll find me down on the London marshes, watching the river rats and their boats (I love their names, all *Ginny*s and *Peg Powler*s). I listen to the hum and crackle of the pylons, watch young men and women jog by red-faced along the towpath, listen to the hoot of coots, and feel at ease.

I read about a condition called Jerusalem Syndrome. Certain people who visit the holy city are just more susceptible to the power of the place. It doesn't matter a bit what religion they claim to be a follower of; anyone can be taken by it. They think they're a messiah, a new god, someone's salvation, that they see things for real for the first time. The place unravels them. Then the Israelis wheel them off to a treatment centre.

The Hollow Shore? It's like that.

*

Jenn and I tried not to talk about what happened to Danny after that evening in the pub.

If the subject ever came up I'd think
life doesn't go in the direction you may have hoped
friends ebb, flow
a ghost may just be delayed understanding
did I let him down?
what now

We decided that too many psychedelics and Danny's pre-existing despondent outlook on life made for a bad combination. When we all became city-dwellers and saw each other only a few times a year – Danny, to his credit, always came to the get-togethers – he'd still talk of the wrecking days and the revenants waving in the fields, the white herons we knew were not there and the booming bird that, I admit, I did hear.

But we didn't want those stories. The past was too painful.

Those things we thought we saw and Danny still claimed he did, they were the fanciful imaginings of young people with fresh itchy tattoos and a green man iconography, with sturdy constitutions able to run on amphetamines, coffee and fags. People with enough hope to still believe that the world was fundamentally a place that could be understood.

Age gave me a gift that Danny was denied; I *know* that there is more to life than what we can perceive. Danny's failing was that he thought he could understand.

The true tragedy of our lives is the knowledge that we don't know.

*

The thing was, the area we came of age did have something funny about it. The old boys with beards who sat in the pubs – Old Neptune, The Black Curlew, The Hollowshore Arms, The Sea Giant, The Son of Cain – would mutter about how the earth we walked on was the body of a fallen giant. Fen went on endlessly of the birds that died out hundreds of years ago but who could still be seen. It was all a matter of perspective, he said. That was the thing that most birders lacked, said Fen: imagination.

In those same pubs, me and Danny picked up the story of the old fisherman with a slate-blank stare and a Tesco shopping bag; see him and your days were numbered.

A phenomenon akin to the Brocken Spectre that made it seem as if a watery and majestic giant was striding out at sea near the horizon.

Our friend who endlessly retold the story of what his father saw out in the woods of Germany and somehow brought back with him. A forest devil, clawed and furred.

Adrianna had her stories of Finland and The Troll Church. We all knew about the whale that washed ashore, bloated and pure. The green hags of England's canals that preyed on the beaten-down.

Somehow, these things all linked together. I knew this, but Danny felt it.

The vampire hunter lived in our town, pedalling its small streets on an antiquated bicycle. He's famous, I remember my mum whispering to me as a kid. I saw him once during the Oyster Festival, standing on the beach just staring at the little ones as they constructed the oyster cairns, shell grottoes lit from within by flickering candlelight. On the Hollow Shore, we had our own way of fending off the darkness, a darkness I could always sense. I saw my friends, my family, the relationships I entered into, as bursts of brief pyrotechnics or slow flickering flame that lit up the endless night. All to be ultimately extinguished, but that was not the point. The fight against the void, that's what life was about. That's what the wrecking days were to me. Our doomed resistance.

Imagination was what could save us, all of us, but it was imagination that stitched Danny up and imagination is easily undone.

I'd go around his place, when we were seventeen years of age, look through his books, an odd collection for a young man. Now, so many years later, I read that stuff myself, but I wonder if it got to him. The relentlessness of it all. All that Blackwood, Machen and Nolan. The nihilist tales about mucoid clowns and vengeful gods. Fucked stories of bad sex and disruptive, uncontrollable desire.

As I aged, I realised all these tales of the fantastic and the bizarre were just reportage. Postcards from the real world. But back then I still believed in realism and a sort of order.

Danny liked pitiless music too. Death metal that fetishised the English landscape, dark electronica and EBM, and the kind of techno that sounded like it was designed to punish a person after they'd already landed in hell. I didn't mind it, but I preferred my ska and punk and reggae and folk, the rave scene of the marshes, music I could dance to without feeling I was stuck inside a cold machine that fed on warm living flesh.

Jenny says that Danny was always going to go the way he went. And I try to argue against any essential pre-determinism in the individual, ask what cruel and fucked-up god would doom a person to their own nature. But I suspect it is true.

When I look at my wife, middle-aged now but still the girl who rested her head in my lap out there on the Hollow Shore, the woman I still love despite the years of marriage, I don't know if I see inevitability or chaos.

*

According to Danny, this is what happened:

You guys had all passed out or had coupled up and were smooching in the undergrowth. I was still as high as a skydancer, I wanted to talk and talk and my heart was fit to burst with how beautiful and mad the world could look. The colours were painful to see. Everything was loaded with meaning, dripping with the stuff. So, I made the only sensible decision: I went for a walk.

Out along the coastal path as the sun was beginning to come up, that half-time when most of humanity is asleep and those who aren't really should be. I just walked and walked, flanking the Swale, thinking of those dead French guys and the birds my dad said he'd seen out on the island. God I'd love to see a spearbird! And for once I felt I was in the right frame of mind to do so. It was all just a matter of perspective.

And then it was like something fell away. Like I'd never known I had poor eyesight until someone slapped a pair of glasses on me. I could see – really see – the Hollow Shore and I knew why we came here and did the things we did.

Ahead of me on the path was an old fisherman whose face I couldn't make out, a wet and muddy Tesco bag hanging from his right hand. At his feet was a white fox that never broke eye contact with me. Which struck me as funny, clichéd almost, you know? Like couldn't this place do better than a weird fox and a ghost?

The old man didn't speak but he sort of beckoned, and as he did my mind was flooded with all the bad shit I'd ever done and I could see the facial expressions of everyone I'd ever let down, I remembered all of the hurt I had felt in my own life, the little bitter reproaches, the cuntish behaviour I endlessly regretted, those times spent in the void with no one to provide a bit of light. And sinking down into the mud to join the Sons of Cain and the French prisoners seemed like such a blessing, enticing, it nearly got me. To sink into the memory of the marsh forever – what sweet relief that would be.

But I resisted. I surprised even myself there. I kept going, knew there was a life still worth fighting for. I thought of all you back there round the fire and how I'd miss you. I thought of my old man looking for his spearbirds. I thought of the wasted lives that lay under the mud across the water.

On I went. The sun was rising in the sky now, but it looked like the sun from the beginning of Watership Down *if you know what I mean? And I hit the fields. There was a path, so I took it and I walked and I walked and that's when I saw them. The revenants.*

Men of straw and sackcloth, women that stank of farmyards and earth and shit and the outdoors. All the bad memories and lost hopes of this shoreline made manifest in a form that seemed appropriate, crudely stitched and coming apart. They were hungry ghosts. The worst of us, the cannibals that hide inside.

As I looked at them, a white heron took flight from somewhere among the dense reed beds and soared over the field. It looked saurian, a proto-bird to swoop down on primitive humans. The straw people just looked at me. There was disappointment, hunger, regret, in their eyes. They started to move towards me.

I ran. Ran and ran until I found you all again and you woke and came out of the undergrowth saying, What the fuck? but I know you saw them too, following me with their shambling run. They saw how many of us there were and that we were friends and something like love existed between us, that we were still alive, and they backed off. Melted back into the fields, scattered like grass on the wind.

You saw them too.

I know you did.

*

I spend the little free time I have finding the dead spots of the city I've called home for twenty years. I'll duck off the High Road, past the Aldi that inhales and exhales shoppers on a rainy Saturday, and head down to the Tottenham Marshes where I can stand under the pylons watching the boaters on the navigation and find a bit of peace.

There, I think about Danny, about what could have happened to him. I remember the wrecking days.

I know that memory is a marsh, and we are all sinking.

Acknowledgements

I'd like to give a big thank you first and foremost to my Influx Press co-conspirators, Kit Caless and Sanya Semakula. Here's to many more adventures!

A massive thanks to Nathan Connolly at Dead Ink for taking a punt on what he described as 'a really weird book'.

Special thanks to Gareth E. Rees for all the bizarre, wonderful, and rain-soaked walks. To Paul Scraton for showing me how very strange the coast can be, whatever country you are in. To Ben Sanders for walking the Hollow Shore with me and showing me some of the wonders of home. To Nina.

I'd like to thank all the amazing writers, editors and publishers I have met over the last six years, who have all provided inspiration and support in some way: Niall Griffiths, Mike Harrison, Nina Allan, Linda Mannheim, David Southwell, Adam Scovell, Simon Spanton, Paul Hawkins, Sarer Scotthorne, George Wielgus, Tom Jeffreys, Chimene Suleyman, Tim Burrows, Luke Turner, Eley Williams, Irenosen Okojie, Dan Duggan, Sam Berkson, Darran Anderson, Sean Preston, Aki Schilz, Helen Marshall, Malcolm Devlin, Tim Jarvis, Peter Haynes, George Sandison, Leila Abu el Hawa, Dan Coxon, Tim Wells, Fernando Sdrigotti, Owen Booth, Aliya Whiteley, Sarah Cleave, Paul Case, Rowena Macdonald, Martin Fuller, Tom Chivers, Ben Myers, Jenn Ashworth, the Ambit crew, the Galley Beggars, everyone at Titan... I could go on for ages.

Thanks to my mum for the books and my dad for the birds.

And finally, up the punx.

Original Publications

Versions of these stories appeared, in slightly different forms, in the following publications:

Saltmarsh (shortlisted for the London Short Story Prize 2015, first published in the *Upshots* anthology)

Breakdown (first published in *The Short Anthology #2)*

Baleen (first published online on Unofficial Britain)

Ren (first published in *The Lonely Crowd #3*)

Greenteeth (first published in *Black Static #80*)

Up and Coming (first published in *PUSH #14/* republished in *PUSH 2* anthology*)*

Knotweed (first published as part of the Galley Beggar Press Singles series)

Shell Grottoes (published online in *InShades Magazine*)

Bent Branches (first published online in *The Cadaverine*)

Coming on Strong (first published in *Prole #14)*

An early version of 'An Exhibition' appeared as 'The Exhibition' in *Connecting Nothing with Something* (Influx Press, 2013)

The Hollow Shore (first published in *Unthology #7*)

Mission Drift (first published in *Under the Radar #13*)

Platforms (published online in *The Jawline Review*)

Brocken Spectre (first published in *Brittle Star #35*)

Tonttukirkko (published by Annexe Publishing)

Spearbird (first published in *Terrain* journal)

Wooden Spoons (published in *The Lonely Crowd*)

Our Own Archipelago (first published in *Panorama Journal*)

We are Nothing but Reeds (first published as part of the *Galley Beggar Singles* series)

The Wrecking Days (previously unpublished)

Publishing the Underground

Publishing the Underground is Dead Ink's way of publishing daring and exciting new fiction from emerging authors. We ask our readers to act as literary patrons and buy our books in advance in order for us to bring them to print. Without this support our books would not be possible.

Dead Ink and the author, Gary Budden, would like to thank all of the following people for generously backing this book – without them this book would not be in your hands.

If you would like to help Dead Ink continue this work please check the website.

www.deadinkbooks.com

Nina Allan

Will Ashon

Jenn Ashworth

Charlotte Bence

Jenny Bernstein

Steve Birt

Alex Blott

SJ Bradley

Siobhan Britton

Dan Brotzel

Kit Caless

Daniel Carpenter

Zelda Chappel

Tracey Connolly

Dan Coxon

Rachel Darling

Jamie Delano

Louise Dickens

Eric Edwards

Laura Emsley

Adrika Anjaria Falcioni

Sam Fisher

Harry Gallon

Sarah Garnham

Daniel Grace

Colin Griffiths

Tina Hagger

Graeme Hall

Paul Hancock

Robin Hargreaves

Francoise Harvey

Felix Haubold

Peter Haynes

David Hebblethwaite

Richard Hirst

Sophie Hopesmith

Rob Jackson

Timothy Jarvis

Tom Jeffreys

Haley Jenkins

Steph Kirkup

Brian Lavelle

Rebecca Lea

Eleanor Lee

Sally Lines

Tony Malone

Wendy Mann

Linda Mannheim

Natalie Marshall
Susan McIvor
Andrew McMillan
Corey Nelson
Irenosen Okojie
Becky Peacock
James Powell
Sean Preston
Floriana Price
Rich Pye
Julie Raby
Meaghan Ralph
Rebecca Read
Gareth Rees
Amber Rollinson
Michael Sabbagh
Tamim Sadikali
George Sandison
Rolf Schröter
Paul Scraton
Anthony Self
Sanya Semakula
Richard Sheehan
Matthew Shenton

Nina Simona
Yvonne Singh
Kieron Smith
Simon Spanton-Walker
Denise Sparrowhawk
Ashley Stokes
Louise Thompson
Luke Turner
Adrian Ward
Paul Watson
Paul Webb
Ben Webster
Aliya Whiteley
George Wielgus
Sandy Wilkie
Eley Williams
Lynne Wilson
Nick Wilson

About Dead Ink...

Dead Ink is a small, ambitious and experimental literary publisher based in Liverpool.

Supported by Arts Council England, we're focused on developing the careers of new and emerging authors.

We believe that there are brilliant authors out there who may not yet be known or commercially viable. We see it as Dead Ink's job to bring the most challenging and experimental new writing out from the underground and present it to our audience in the most beautiful way possible.

Our readers form an integral part of our team. You don't simply buy a Dead Ink book, you invest in the authors and the books you love.

About the Author...

Gary Budden writes fiction and creative non-fiction about the intersections of British sub-culture, landscape, psychogeography, hidden history, nature, horror, weird fiction and more. A lot of it falls under the banner 'landscape punk'.

His work has appeared in Black Static, Unthology, Year's Best Weird Fiction, The Lonely Crowd, Litro, Structo, The Quietus and many more. His story 'Greenteeth' was nominated for a 2017 British Fantasy Award and adapted into a short film by the filmmaker Adam Scovell. He also co-runs indie publisher Influx Press.

@gary_budden
www.newlexicons.com